Against The Odds

J. Adams

Against The Odds

J. Adams

J. Adams

Against the Odds 2nd Edition
Copyright © 2011, 2014 J. Adams
Jewel of the West Publishing
All Rights Reserved
ISBN-13: 978-0615457369
ISBN-10: 0615457363

Library of Congress Control Number: 2011903397

Cover design by Laura J Miller
anaurthorsart.com

Jewel of the West™
P U B L I S H I N G

Against The Odds

J. Adams

To every woman who has ever reached for something better and defied the odds to achieve it. This one is for you!

J. Adams

A heart is never truly restless until Love enters the equation. Of course, when this intense sentiment materializes, odds are, you will find that the wretched internal organ was only sleeping.

J. A.

J. Adams

Hard-won freedom is priceless.

Atlanta, GA

I was angry. No, correction, I was livid! But more than anything, I was just plain tired.

"Sign them," I said, tossing the folded divorce papers on the desk.

When Jerome looked up at me, I saw a mixture of incredulity, arrogance, and even a little sorrow play across his features. He stood and came around the desk.

"Raine," he said, drawing out my name in the whiny way that had grown to be completely annoying a long time ago. "Come on, girl. You don't want to do this."

I knew that same old tired line was coming, but it still amazed me that he was continuing to hang on, even when there was absolutely nothing left to hang on to. I stood silently for a moment, allowing my eyes to roam from his expensive Italian loafers, up his dark gray, double-breasted three-piece suit, crisp white shirt and silk tie, finally resting my gaze on what I once thought was a handsome face.

I took in his smooth, dark skin and immaculately trimmed hair. Not able to help it, my thoughts went back to a time when I thought he was the most amazing black man in the world. I was eighteen, fresh out of high school, young and naive. He was smooth, he was sharp, and he was sexy.

None of these things should have been the basis for marriage, but sadly, for me they were. Oh, I knew it had been more lust than love. Still, when Jerome proposed to me over seven years ago during a candle-lit dinner in his Peachtree Towers office, I had accepted. I had been mesmerized by his money, his power, and his position, which he used to help me get into Zuri, one of the top modeling agencies in Atlanta. Everything seemed right with the world when I was with him. And he was pleased to have me adorning his arm at the many social functions we attended.

Through the years I grew to care about him very deeply. I thought I might even love him. Then came Jerome's first indiscretion, which as it turned out, was the beginning of the end for me. I forgave him for that act of infidelity. I even forgave him for the second one that occurred a year later. But this latest one . . . Shuniqua, this hoochie of a home-wrecker who I had even entertained at our backyard parties on several occasions, was more than I could stomach. I was tired of forgiving and forgetting. The forgiving fountain had run completely dry. I mean, good grief, we hadn't even slept in the same bed in over six months because of his decision to seek intimacy elsewhere. Our sham of a marriage should have ended a long time ago. I had tried to end it, but Jerome kept holding on. Why, I didn't know. He sure made me feel worthless enough. All I seem to be good for now was decoration. In another few years my looks would begin to fade. Then what? I would most likely wait to be tossed aside like a worn pair of jeans that had seen better days. In some ways I felt like that now, worn and weary. He had used up the best of me, and I didn't know if there was much of me left to ever give to anyone else, or if I could even allow that to happen.

Pulling my mind forward, I sighed and tried to rid myself of the depressing thoughts. "You know what, Jerome? I *do* want to do this." I tapped my manicured nails on the desk next to a framed photo of the two of us. It was taken last year during a Caribbean vacation Jerome took me on to make up for his previous act of infidelity. To anyone looking at the photo, we looked like the perfect couple, so in love and so into each other. It was very deceiving. Our whole marriage was a lie.

"Just sign the papers."

He sat on the edge of the desk and reached for my hand. I moved away abruptly. "Come on now, Raine. You know that girl don't mean nothing to me."

I couldn't stop the throaty chuckle from escaping me. "That girl, huh? Does Shuniqua know she's just that girl? Did you tell her straight up she doesn't mean anything?" When he looked away, I added, "Humph. Well, I guess you had better tell her that. Only don't do it on my account, because this bank is closed."

"Raine, you and I have been together a long time. We have too much history to just give up."

I shifted my feet impatiently and began tapping a velvet black pump on the tile floor. "Give up what? There's nothing holy about this matrimony anymore. Your actions caused that term to wither away a long time ago, and I'm tired of letting things slide."

I have always been good at keeping my voice level and my emotions in check. Through the years I even managed to control the involuntary neck roll that usually accompanied my 'getting some attitude' emotion, but now all that practiced control was slipping, and the desire to rein it in was gone. Gone just like my feelings for him.

I pushed a long spiraled lock of hair behind my ear and placed my hands on my hips, slightly crinkling my designer suit.

"I'm tired, Jerome," I repeated again. "I'm tired of playing Mrs. Jerome Edmunds. I'm ready to be Miss Raine Allen again." I looked at him intently. "You know what? I've got proof. I've got lawyers. I've got the money and the time to take your sorry behind to the cleaners if I have to. So just sign the damn papers and let me be!"

Having said the magic phrase-specifically the one to do with his money-I finally got the desired effect. I watched his shoulders sag in defeat as he picked the papers up from the desk. He took an expensive silver pen from his coat pocket-the silver pen I bought for him, I might add-flipped through the papers, and added his signature.

I sighed inwardly, a feeling of victorious freedom filling me, breathing life back into a heart that had been completely bled dry.

Jerome handed the papers to me, then sat back on the desk and folded his arms. "So, I guess your attorney will be in touch with mine to go over things."

I folded the papers and put them in my purse. "Yes, he will."

He was quiet for a moment, his eyes roaming the length of me. "I'm sorry, Raine. I messed up . . . I'm sorry."

"So am I."

He rubbed his smooth chin. "What are your plans now?"

I smiled and walked to the door, pausing with my hand on the knob. "Caroline and David McKade have invited me to come out and spend some time with them."

He grinned. "So you're going to just leave everything and move to New Mexico? Girl, give me a break. That's white man's land for sure. You'll be back here before you know it. That ain't your kind of life."

I turned back to face him fully. "Have you

forgotten Caroline and David *are* white? Their skin color never seemed to matter to you when you were handling some of their investments."

"That's because money is the same color no matter whose hand it's in."

I shook my head but didn't comment. I wasn't about to touch that one.

"What about your mama? You know she's going to have a fit."

"Mama will understand." I snorted. "I'm sure of that." I again turned to leave.

"Well, what about your contract with Zuri?"

You're reaching, Jerome. "I only have a few months left and I'm done." I looked at him intently. "Completely."

"So, this is how it's gonna be, huh? No hug or kiss goodbye?"

"You gave all of that up the moment you went to Shuniqua's bed."

"Why you being so cold?"

I again shook my head and opened the door. "Have a good life, Jerome. If you can, that is."

"Don't worry, I will. You just go on running from yours."

I chuckled inwardly, thinking how quickly he'd mashed out his earlier apology. "I'm not running *from* my life, Jerome. I'm running to it."

Against The Odds

Change is an adventure.

One

Six months later
Roswell, New Mexico

I can't believe I'm really in *alien* territory," I joked, sitting across from Caroline.

She laughed and handed me a glass of cold lemonade. "Yeah, right. The closest we ever get to aliens is when some of the ranch hands come back to work after a weekend of drinking and carousing around the valley. They're usually so green, they look like aliens. And just between you and me, that's when David slams the bunkhouse door the hardest."

I smiled, loving her sense of humor. "It serves them right." Sighing, I sipped my lemonade. "I've missed you so much, Caroline."

"I've missed you too, Raine. I've even missed Atlanta a little, if you can believe that." She smiled.

"We hated moving, but when David's father died, the ranch went to David and his brother, Hayden, so we had to leave. I'm sure Hayden could have handled the place alone, but it was half David's responsibility too, and he felt obligated to come." She gazed through the kitchen window across the land. "Now I'm glad we came. I love it here."

I quietly stared out the window as my thoughts drifted back to the first time I met Caroline and David. Jerome was hosting a party at his office for both his new and prospective clients. Caroline and David were in the process of making a final decision about Jerome's company handling some of their investments. They were being wined and dined by Jerome and his staff to solidify the deal. I connected with Caroline immediately and we were soon the best of friends.

Jerome and I saw quite a bit of the couple after that. Though Jerome and David had nothing in common, they got along well and the friendship was good. Good that is until David and Caroline moved away, taking their money with them. Caroline and I remained close, but Jerome had no use for them after that. Of course that was always the way with Jerome.

Pulling my thoughts to the present, I observed Caroline for a moment, taking in her youthful, motherly smile. There were streaks of gray in her dark hair and deep lines appeared around her blue eyes when she smiled, but she had gained an earthy beauty that wasn't there before. And it only added to the regal gracefulness she had always possessed. "I think this life suits you," I finally said.

"Well, what about you?" she asked with a grin. "You've only been here for a week and just look at you! With that beautiful curly mane of yours pulled back and you walking around in Wranglers and boots, girl, you're already wearing this life well, too."

Grinning, I looked down at my hands. After a week of helping Caroline with work around the house, my perfect manicure wasn't perfect anymore. Gone were the designer clothes and shoes. They were now replaced by feminine plaid shirts, t-shirts, jeans, and western boots. Also gone was the heavy makeup. Now my light brown eyes were only adorned with a little eyeliner and mascara, and my lips touched with clear gloss.

After studying these changes in the mirror earlier that morning, I decided I liked them. I liked them a lot. Having been a very busy model for five years and being made up daily, this more natural look was a refreshing change for me. Besides, walking away from that life was no sacrifice. I had done well. Now I was done, period.

Most of the people in Atlanta who knew me couldn't believe or understand my decision to leave it all and walk away. Sometimes I still found it hard to believe myself. To everyone that knew me, I had everything. And for a short while, I believed that as well.

All my life I had dreamed of being a model. I wanted the glamor and the glitz that came with it. Not to mention the money. But I never dreamed of the complications that would come with that life. When I was younger I thought, *This is how I'm going to make my mark on the world.* Had it been worth it? Maybe. Had it brought me happiness? Some. But in the grand scheme of things, I knew now that none of it mattered. It was all insignificant to what was really important. A family, something I could call my own. That's what was important to me. I thought I'd had that with Jerome. As unfaithful as he had been, I had been willing to keep trying. But it turned out those things weren't important to him. Truthfully, I think I had known that all along, but I let myself be strung along for the ride because of what a life with him would give me. A supposed family and financial security. I thought I could have it all, but it eventually became too much. The lies and deceit had drowned what feelings I had for him and washed them away like a sandcastle on a beach. I finally grew up.

I again looked down at my hands. I thought about Jerome and couldn't help but smile as I contemplated what he would think if he saw me now. I would get a kick out of his reaction to be sure. His black Barbie doll was history.

Caroline must have read my thoughts in my expression. "Raine, that man is a horse's hind end to treat you the way he did. I think if he was here now, I'd strap him to the back of one and let it drag his tail up and down this valley. Goodness knows he deserves it."

I covered my mouth, laughing out loud. "The

closest you will ever get Jerome to a horse is watching a race from the comfort of his leather recliner. And that's only if he has a bet riding on it."

She chuckled a moment, shaking her head, her straight hair tumbling around her shoulders. Then she sobered and looked at me intently. "So, how are you really?" she asked earnestly.

"I'm doing okay. You know it had been a long time coming. Our marriage was over long before I got his John Hancock on the papers."

"I know. And I keep thinking that in a way, it's good you didn't have any children."

"I do, too," I agreed with a sigh. "But it wasn't from lack of trying, at least on my part."

"I know that, too." Caroline took a drink from her glass. "Maybe it wasn't in the cards for you and Jerome. Or, maybe it just wasn't the time."

"Well, either way, I can see now that a child wouldn't have made much difference in our relationship. As much as I wanted to be a mother, and still want to be one day, it sure wouldn't be good for a child to be in this situation now, being pulled back and forth between divorced parents. I know it happens, but it's still a sad way to grow up."

We sat for a moment in silence as I pondered that thought. Truthfully, I really did feel grateful now that there were no kids between us. As unfaithful as Jerome had been in our marriage, any child of ours would most likely have a brother or sister or two running around somewhere in Atlanta. That would have been all I needed. To have one of Jerome's illegitimate children knocking on my door one day looking for his *daddy*.

I closed my eyes and shook my head as feelings of anger slowly entered me again. "Unfaithful jerk!" I muttered softly.

Caroline's snicker drew me from my thoughts. "All right, girl. Come back to Roswell."

I smiled. "I'm here. Just doing some therapeutic reminiscing. Purely therapy."

Against The Odds

Opening one's eyes can clear the view.

Two

I walked around the ranch again with Caroline, wanting to familiarize myself with the things they did there daily. It was a beautiful piece of land. Gazing out into the distance, there were red rock mountains as far as the eye could see. A sea of alfalfa swayed in the breeze blowing across the endless acres, and dots of yellow wildflowers toiled in the shimmering waves of green. To my left and out a ways, I could see a herd of cattle grazing. Further out in front of me, there was a corral. At the moment it was occupied by one of the hired hands walking a horse.

I turned and looked back up at the house, admiring the colorful flower boxes Caroline planted that lined the upper and lower back windows, filled with red, purple, and pink geraniums. I smiled. It might be a ranch, but Caroline had seen to it that a woman's touch was apparent.

As we continued walking, I listened to Caroline as she rattled off the names of the men working for them and what they did. She told me that most of the men worked from sunup to sundown because there was always so much to do, but they enjoyed the work. She said it would be good if I got to know them.

"I will eventually," I said as Caroline waved to a couple of hands loading the back of a truck with bales of hay. They both smiled and waved back, pausing in their work as we walked by.

"I do believe you have a fan club," Caroline said, grinning.

"Yeah, right," I casually shot back, casting my eyes downward, trying to ignore the stares of the two men.

Caroline placed a gentle hand on my arm and I stopped, turning to her. She looked at me quietly for a few seconds and smiled. "I know you've had a rough time of it, Raine, but keep your heart open, okay? Don't let one man's stupidity ruin it for all men. There's someone out there for you. I know there is. Just keep your heart open."

Wrapping my arms around my middle, I looked out across the land again. "That's easier said than done, girlfriend. And I'm not ready to think about it just yet."

"That's all right," she said, putting her arm around my shoulders. "You'll know when you're ready. Just stay open to the possibility."

"I'll try," I replied with a smile, thinking of the

future. I was still young. There would be time. Just not right now.

We were just making our way past the bunkhouse when David came out.

"Hey there, gorgeous," he called to Caroline as he walked out to us. He pulled her close for a kiss. Her smile was wide as she went into her husband's embrace.

I silently watched the two. When David released her, I noticed a few drops of sweat rolling down his face, continuing down his chest where his shirt hung unbuttoned. His hands and face were dirty, but it didn't seem to bother Caroline. I couldn't say that I blamed her. Even with sweat and grime covering him, David was a good looking man. He was tall and still very muscular for his age. His grayish-blond hair hung down to his collar, and his clean-shaven face, already showing signs of a five o'clock shadow, housed deep blue eyes framed by thick bushy brows. I was sure he was probably quite the catch in his younger days. Caroline had shown me a few pictures of their son who was now in his late twenties and a sergeant in the Marines. The photos definitely gave me a glimpse of what David probably looked like at that age.

My heart warmed as I watched David smile lovingly at his wife. The affection the two still showed to one another was a little awe-inspiring. He walked over to me and casually draped an arm around my shoulders.

"So, what do you think about our simple life out

here?"

"Well, it beats the smog and bog of Atlanta. And besides, I'd take the sound of calves bawling over the whine of Jerome calling my name any day."

David laughed. "Well, you came to the right place to celebrate your new-found freedom. And speaking of freedom, I've got to get back down to the stable. Sally's having a hard time trying to deliver that foal. It's trying to come breech."

"Oh, no!" Caroline said sadly. Sally was her favorite mare. "Oh, come on, Raine. Let's go down." She turned to her husband. "It's all right, isn't it?"

"Yeah," he said and looked at me. "Normally we'd stay away because it would slow her progress, but since we have to be there anyway, it's fine. Besides, this will be an experience you will never forget, Raine."

"That's what I'm afraid of," I said with a smile.

"You'll love it," David assured me. He turned to Caroline. "Hayden got back late last night from purchasing some horses in Evanston. He's in the stable with Sally. She's in good hands with him, so don't worry."

"So, I finally get to meet the famous Hayden," I interjected. I had heard so much about the unseen man, I began to think he was a myth.

"Yeah, he was completely beat when he got in last night and went straight to his place."

"His place?" I questioned. "I thought *this* was his place, too."

"It is," Caroline said, taking her husband's

offered arm. "He just felt he needed his own space, which we could understand. He has his own house on the property. It's nice to still have him close."

David grinned at his wife. "Shoot, sugar, you know that boy ain't going nowhere. This ranch is in his blood."

"You got that right." She pointed to a house in the distance. It was shaded by a small grove of trees. "Hayden built that house himself last year. I'll take you over there later to see it. It's beautiful."

I made a soft noise of approval. "I look forward to it."

Life is full of amazing discoveries, but only when you take the time to live it.

Three

By the time we reached the stable, Sally's foal was halfway into the world. There were two men working on the horse, both of them shirtless. One of the men had his back to us, pulling on the hind legs of the colt, and there was a blood-tinged film covering his arms and hands. Caroline and I stayed out of the way so the men could work. As I took in the dimly-lit surroundings, I was quickly overwhelmed by the smell of horses, leather, and straw.

"How's she doing?" David asked the man with his back to us as he changed places with the other worker.

"Just about here," came the deep drawl of the man as he worked to bring the little foal safely into the world.

There was a quiet tenseness in the air, but as the

nameless cowboy continued to work, I soon found that my fascination was divided between him and the birth of the foal. I couldn't help noticing the way the muscles of his broad, tanned back rippled and the way his large biceps flexed as he coaxed the new babe out. Never in my life had I ever seen a more sculpted man, not even among the construction workers my friends and I would casually admire as we walked by building sites in downtown Atlanta. When the man turned his head slightly, I saw that his neatly trimmed beard and mustache matched his tousled, thick chestnut-brown hair, which was streaked with golden highlights and hung down to his shoulders. He looked to me to be a large man, one that I wouldn't care to encounter in a dark alleyway, but at the same time, I could also picture him on the front of a western romance novel.

Both David and the cowboy took a deep breath when the foal was finally delivered. I heaved a relieved sigh as well. Watching it all had been pretty amazing and the experience left me in awe of life and its creations. It truly was something I would never forget.

While the third man took care of mother and child, David and the cowboy stood and walked over to a large metal tub to wash up. A beam of sunlight came through a crack in the ceiling of the barn. It reflected off the large belt buckle that stood out on the cowboy's narrow waist.

Caroline took my arm and we approached him. "Hayden," she said as the tall man toweled off his massive arms and sculpted chest and stomach. "I'd like you to meet my good friend, Raine Allen. We became friends in Atlanta and she has come to stay for a while."

He nodded toward me, his thick, tousled locks falling against the sides of his face. "Nice to meet you," he said, pushing a hand back through his hair.

So, this is Hayden. "It's good to meet you, too." Now that I was looking at him, I could definitely see his resemblance to David.

Hayden quietly looked down at me for another moment, unsettling me with his gray eyes. And I didn't like being unsettled. I didn't like the feeling at all, and I was surprised by my internal reaction to his gaze.

He finally turned to his brother. "I'm gonna run and haul that hay on over to Dale's place. Be back in an hour or so."

"All right. Tell him I'll bring the other mare back over there later. Her leg has healed up pretty well."

Hayden put his shirt back on and placed a worn, brown western hat on his head. He looked down at me once more and tipped his hat. When I smiled and nodded, he turned to leave.

Good grief, that's a bear of a man! I thought as I watched his giant yet perfect frame walking away. Caroline had mentioned that he was in his early thirties, but his size made it seem like *he* should be the older brother instead of David.

Caroline's voice interrupted my musings. "Hey, Hayden, wait up!" she called as she quickly moved past me to catch up to him.

I stood by the stable entrance and waited for Caroline as she talked with her brother-in-law. I was startled when he glanced back at me and wordlessly nodded to her before turning and walking away. Caroline headed back in my direction. Just then, David came up behind me and draped his arm around my shoulders, a sly grin on his face.

"I think Caroline's getting ready to jar a couple of pears."

"She's what?" I asked, somewhat bewildered.

David chuckled. "Never mind."

Caroline looped my arm through hers and we headed back to the house.

"Raine, I asked Hayden if he wouldn't mind taking you with him, just so you can get out for a bit."

I stopped and looked at her, suddenly speechless. "But . . . Caroline, I don't even know him."

She waved a hand through the air, brushing off my response. "Oh, don't worry about that. Hayden is easy to get to know. Once he warms up to a person, he's good company. You'll enjoy the drive."

"But I thought we were going to go out later," I continued to protest. I wasn't comfortable with the idea of going for a drive with a total stranger, even if he was David's brother. And I felt slightly annoyed at Caroline for putting me in this position.

For the most part, I considered myself a very

outgoing person and I usually welcomed opportunities to get to know people, so I didn't know why going for a ride with my friend's brother-in law bothered me so much, but it did.

Caroline squeezed my arm softly. "You'll be in good hands with Hayden, Raine. And we can still go out later if you want to."

Taking in her adamant expression I finally shrugged my shoulders in defeat, thinking that it really would be nice to get out for a while. "Okay, I'll go, but only if Hayden doesn't mind."

"He doesn't mind at all," Caroline assured me. "He'll be back in just a few minutes to pick you up."

As I went into the house to grab my purse, I found myself for the first time in my life wondering what I could talk about for the next hour with a total stranger. Unfortunately, I couldn't come up with a single thing.

Surprises always come with the start of something new.

Four

It's amazing how one's opinion can change in a short time with just a little bit of effort.

As Hayden pulled his metallic gray Chevy truck back out onto the road exiting Dale Reed's farm, I couldn't help smiling as I contemplated how different I felt during the drive there than I felt now.

Not much had been said between Hayden and me as we drove out to the Reed farm to deliver the hay. He had asked me about myself and I told him a little about my life in Georgia, my modeling career, and some of my interests. When I in turn asked him about himself, his reply had come in two or three sentences, all of them referring to his work on the ranch, and that was it. He had said nothing about himself personally. But I figured what little conversation I managed to get out of him was better than if we were just discussing the weather, though it might have produced a sentence or two more.

When we'd reached our destination, I remained in the truck while he and the older man, who I assumed to be Dale, unloaded the back. There was no introduction. Neither was there much conversation between the two men, but I did notice Dale occasionally glancing at me. I couldn't help smiling at his obvious curiosity.

After another moment, I took a deep breath and slipped into my bold mode. I got out of the truck, walked back to where they were unloading the hay and introduced myself. I could tell by the look on the man's weathered face that my action had been unexpected. Judging by the look on Hayden's face, I'd caught him by surprise as well. When I put out my hand, the man took off his glove and shook it.

"It's good to meet you, Raine. I'm Dale."

"It's a pleasure to meet you, too," I said back. I moved out of the way to let them finish unloading the hay.

While they worked, Dale asked me the usual questions. Where was I from? How long would I be here? And how was I enjoying my visit? I found it amusing that I had gotten more conversation from him in just two minutes than I had in the twenty minutes I had spent with Hayden. I mentally chalked it up to Hayden just being a listener. Maybe he wasn't much of a talker.

Once they finished, Dale handed us a couple of

Cokes from the cooler on the porch and paid Hayden. We thanked him and got back into the truck.

And now here we were, back on the road again.

The day was very warm and the cloudless sky was bright. As we drove toward the sun, I slipped on a pair of sunglasses and savored the breeze coming through the open windows as it whipped the billowing curls that had escaped my ponytail. Red mountains loomed in every direction and there wasn't a tree in sight. Having moved from a state where you couldn't see the forest for the trees, this was definitely different. The tree covered valleys at home were beautiful, but New Mexico was also beautiful in its own way, and the dry heat was a welcome change from the humidity of Georgia. At least now when I dried off after a shower in the mornings I actually *felt* dry.

I turned on the seat slightly so I was facing the silent cowboy a little. I took in the faded blue t-shirt he wore, which stretched and hugged his massive, muscular form. I mused that the mold must have been broken after he was created. His physique was absolutely incredible.

"Thanks for bringing me with you."

He tipped his hat back some. "You're welcome." He looked at me and smiled slightly. "I think old Dale's gone sweet on ya."

I chuckled. "Oh, really?"

He nodded. "I ain't never heard him talk so much."

I snorted. *Listen to who's talking.*

As if he'd read my thoughts, he said, "Maybe he was just trying to keep up with me in conversation."

When I comically arched a brow, he grinned and I couldn't help grinning in return. His already handsome face was instantly transformed. His gray eyes sparkled and he suddenly seemed so much more approachable. True, he had the looks of some giant western god, rugged and strong, but now I actually felt comfortable with him. Caroline was right. He really was good company.

"Hey," Hayden said, pulling me from my musings. "You wanna see something fun?"

I smiled at his sudden boldness. "Sure. I'd love to."

He smiled back and turned his truck toward town.

Sometimes friendship is found where least expected and when it is needed most.

Five

"You have got to be kidding me," I mused out loud as we toured the International UFO Museum.

Hayden chuckled. "I know, I know," he drawled. "Our biggest claim to fame is also the most ridiculous thing ever heard of."

"Oh, I don't know. Caroline told me some of the hired hands look like these little guys after a weekend of partying," I joked, looking at a replica of one of the little green men. I took in the large, colorful mural behind it, depicting a flying saucer crashing to the earth.

"She's got that right." He grinned slyly. "When I was younger, *my* skin took on that color a time or two."

"But you're older and wiser now, right?"

He rubbed the back of his neck. "Daddy didn't take too kindly to my drinking, so I gave it up. Haven't had a drop since I was nineteen."

"Good for you," I said, enjoying hearing something about him that wasn't related to the ranch. It was nice to hear him opening up a little more.

Hayden told me his drinking had most likely stemmed from losing his mother. He was only twelve when his mother died from cancer. It was hard for him and David. But since David was already grown and out on his own, David had been able to handle their mother's death a little better. Their father had raised Hayden alone. Hayden told me how much he loved his father and that he was a good man. I told him his father would be very proud of him for what he had accomplished and for the kind of man he had become. He thanked me for the compliment. Then I shared with him how much I missed having a father in my life when I was younger. I knew my mother had done the best she could to raise me properly, and she always made sure I never went without. Still, it would have been nice to have a father figure. Of course, in my neck of the woods, having an absent father was standard. We probably could have started a club.

Entering another room of the museum, I snorted derisively as we viewed a model of the notorious alien autopsy. "Oh, now this is priceless."

"Ain't it though? Now you can't get more authentic than that."

"No, I don't think you can," I said with a laugh.

After walking around for a little while longer, he asked, "Are you hungry?"

"A little," I answered, looking up at him. I had to tip my head back to look at his face. Five-feet-ten is pretty tall for a woman, and I had been around my share of tall men, but Hayden had to be close to seven feet.

"You like seafood?"

"I love it."

"Well, I know it will be hard, but do you think you can tear yourself away from this fascinating medical procedure to go and get a bite?"

I grinned. "If I really have to."

We settled into a booth at *Red Lobster* and quickly ordered our meals. I had eaten at the restaurant quite a bit in Atlanta, and despite Jerome's aversion to what he considered too low a class of dining for his taste, it was one of my favorite places to eat. It was also Mama's favorite. You would think that dining there in Roswell without her would make me a little homesick, but it didn't. Of course, the company I was keeping at the moment helped.

Soon the waitress delivered our food and refilled our water glasses, lingering over Hayden as she did. I choked back a snort as I watched our loose goose in action. Now *that* was something universal; you zero in on the target and work the so-called assets to the best of your ability, and believe me, she was working them. I shook my head slightly. It was the same everywhere.

After the slow refilling of our glasses, she finally left us to our meals.

As we ate and talked, I couldn't help glancing around at the people in the dining area. They were all so different, yet they seemed so down to earth, so laid back. No one was in a hurry. And I could count the designer dresses and three-piece suits on one hand. The little city seemed to move at its own pace. After living such a rushed life for so long, this was a nice change.

After a while, I finally became so full I pushed my plate away. I leaned back and sighed. "I swear, if I eat another bite, my jeans will split at the seams."

"I doubt that," Hayden said with a grin, leaning back. "I don't think a person can get any littler than you are."

I turned in my seat and leaned back against the wall, stretching my legs across the booth seat and arched an eyebrow. "I don't know if I should take that as a compliment or an insult."

"It was a compliment." One corner of his full mouth twitched slightly. "Just don't get any smaller or you might disappear all together."

When he grinned, I took a piece of ice from my cup and threw it at him. As expected, he dodged and I missed.

"You're dangerous, darlin'," he said with a laugh. "I'll have to be careful what I say around you from now on."

"Yes, you will," I said, grinning back. Then I heaved a sobering sigh. "When it comes to the subject of my weight, I throw myself a pity-party from time to time."

"What do you mean?"

"Well, truthfully, I've never been on a diet or had to watch what I eat like most models I know. Sometimes it's a blessing, sometimes a curse." I paused, becoming thoughtful. "When I was younger, my mother took me to the doctor and had me checked out because she couldn't seem to get me fattened up, no matter what she fed me. I don't know why it bothered her so much, but it did. I guess since I was her only child she was more protective." I shook my head slightly. "I was a scrawny kid and a scrawny teenager." I smiled. "Busty but scrawny."

Hayden smiled back but didn't comment. "So, what did the doctor say?"

"He told her there was absolutely nothing wrong with me. My metabolism had always run through the roof. It still does. But sometimes I do feel like it would be nice to put on a few pounds. I guess the grass is always greener elsewhere, huh?"

Hayden leaned forward and again smiled, his eyes intently looking into mine. "I think you're fine just the way you are."

"Thank you." I was warmed by his compliment.

"So," he said, leaning back, "you want another tour of the museum before we go? Or would you rather go looking for signs of alien visitation?"

I laughed. "I think I've had all the extraterrestrial enlightenment I can handle right now."

"Awww," he drawled, feigning disappointment. "I was looking forward to driving you out to the desert and finding some of them little footprints. I brought aluminum foil for our heads and everything."

I snorted, then laughed. "You, in aluminum foil? Now I would definitely pay to see that."

He chuckled. "You and the rest of the hands at the ranch."

"Now that *would* be priceless."

"Darlin', even a mental picture of it is more than I can take."

We looked at each other silently for a moment and broke up laughing all over again.

"I think we'd best get out of here before they throw us out."

"I think you're right," I agreed, still chuckling.

We talked for another few minutes and stood to leave. I thanked Hayden again for taking me out. He said he was happy to do it.

And judging by the look of amusement still lingering in his eyes, I knew the day had been just as fun for him as it had been for me.

The simple things in life are the ones that bring the most joy.

Six

Early one morning of the following week, Hayden found me by the hen house. I smiled widely, a feeling of accomplishment filling me at having gathered the eggs without any help. Caroline had shown me how it was done the day before. And now here I stood, a basket of fresh eggs hanging from my arm. I was proud of myself. Hayden told me he was proud of me too. He said he was looking forward to having some of the eggs for breakfast the next day, wanting to taste some of the fruits of my labor. I told him it was more the hens' labor than mine.

With each new day I became more amazed at myself over how much I was changing. I found that I didn't miss the city at all. Not one bit. I deeply enjoyed this new life and everything about it. I enjoyed the work and the challenges of doing new things. But more than anything, I enjoyed waking up to the sound of people in the house. Caroline and David treated me like a member of their family. They included me in everything. Caroline had even let me prepare breakfast the previous morning. I was grateful to her for allowing me to make myself more useful.

In all the years of pursuing a modeling career and living the high life while enduring a loveless marriage, I had missed out on so many things. I missed out on living. But then again, I was never still long enough to even know.

Now I was learning to enjoy the simple things in life more. Things like the sound of birds chirping, watching a sunrise, a sunset, and even the pleasure of sitting under a shady tree silently enjoying a glass of lemonade. For the first time in my life I enjoyed little moments of contemplation and meditation. I was becoming like most of the people in Roswell. I was in no hurry to get anywhere, and I actually took the time to relax and take mental pictures of the world around me. Even something as simple as tying a quilt with Caroline and one of her friends, or helping to bottle fresh peaches added to this new level of contentment in my life. I was now doing meaningful things.

And of course, Hayden was always near with a warm smile and a sincere compliment for all my efforts. He was a good friend, and it was nice to feel appreciated for a change.

I spent that afternoon on the phone with Mama. It was so good to talk to her. She was truly the only thing I missed in Atlanta. I had no siblings and there was no other family to speak of, just Mama.

I knew Mama had been disappointed in my decision to leave because she was so used to having me close, and it didn't help that Jerome was rubbing my 'desertion' in her face every chance he got. But I also knew that Mama understood. She knew what it was like to have to deal with an unfaithful man. She knew the heartache of having to make the decision I did. She knew the questions every woman who has ever been in that situation has to ask.

Do you turn your head away and just let things go on or do you finally take a stand and say no more? Do you continue to be walked over or do you finally begin to respect yourself?

Mama had been faced with that decision with my own father. It had been hard, but she chose to respect herself and end the charade. That fact alone made the bond she and I shared that much stronger, spanning the miles between us and strengthening our connection.

Sometimes it still pained me to think about what Mama went through. She had been forced to endure my father's late nights, as well as the phone calls that would mysteriously and automatically result in an abrupt dial tone when she answered the phone. She had endured the stress and whispers of the neighborhood, yet she always held her head up high. She has always been an inspiration to me.

Little did I know I would one day find myself in the same situation . . . but there was one major difference; Mama truly loved Daddy, heart and soul. She truly deserved happiness. My own decision to marry hadn't been motivated by real love, a fact that I will always regret. And now I was facing the consequences of that choice. I suddenly wondered if I would ever know real love. Did I even know what real love was? Would I know it when it came? *If* it came? This was a department I was sorely lacking in.

Rein it in, girl, I mentally scolded.

Abruptly ending another pity-party, I again gave my full attention to my mother.

Mama was once again filled with questions. How are Caroline and David? How are things going for me? Am I happy? She put more emphasis on the last question.

I told her the change had been good for me and I was happier than I had been in a long time. Surprisingly, my answer seemed to satisfy her. I told her that I missed her and suggested that she come out for a visit. She promised me she would think about it. We talked a few minutes longer.

Before ending the call, I felt the need to apologize to Mama for Jerome's behavior. I couldn't understand why he felt the need to annoy her. Mama said she was glad I had moved away because Jerome wouldn't have left me alone had I stayed. Even now he was still an unwanted part of my life because he was annoying my mother. He knew it would bother me, and it did. Still, I wouldn't give him the satisfaction of knowing just *how much* it bothered me.

I again urged Mama to come out to Roswell and again she said she would think about it. Then I told her I loved her and we hung up. I smiled as I thought about our conversation and decided to make getting Mama to come out for a visit my goal.

Hayden called from his place that evening and told Caroline he wouldn't be there for dinner. It seemed the drain under his kitchen sink was leaking and he was trying to fix it. So Caroline dished him up a plate of food and sent me to deliver it.

Even though his house could be seen through the trees in the distance, it was still too far to walk with a plate of food and get it to him warm, so I drove David's truck. I had only been to Hayden's once. Caroline had taken me over to see the place after Hayden and I got back from our unforgettable outing at the UFO Museum.

Hayden's home was beautiful. It was a colonial-style brick home with white siding and black shutters on the windows. It boasted a three-car garage, which he never used. There was a large white vinyl deck on the back that wrapped around the side of the house to make a lovely veranda. There was even a vinyl porch swing.

I knocked on the screen door lightly. A minute later Hayden appeared, his tall, massive, shirtless form filling the doorway, a smile on his face. I was startled at the sudden feel of unwanted goose-bumps on my arms at the sight of him. I mentally put myself in check.

"Hey there," he said, opening the screen door and moving aside so I could enter.

"Hey, yourself. I just came to bring you some dinner." I grinned slyly. "We wouldn't want you to starve."

He grinned back. "Good thing I've got ya'll looking out for me." He took the plate of food. "Mmmm, smells good. Thank you."

"You're welcome."

"Come on in the kitchen."

I followed him through the house, again take in the beautiful interior.

Hayden didn't have much as far as decor, but the combination of the rustic leather and fabric furniture set off by hard wood floors, made it homey and inviting.

As I entered the kitchen, I was freshly awed by the large, stained pine-wood table and six matching chairs. The table was bare, as were the walls in the kitchen, but it was still lovely. I noticed various tools scattered on the floor in front of the sink. The cabinet doors were open and an old towel was lying beneath the drain pipe.

Hayden put the plate of food on the table. "Have a seat," he said, pulling out a chair for me. Then he went back over to the sink. "I managed to get it fixed." He knelt down and wiped up the excess water with the towel. Having finished, he grabbed a fork from the drawer, sat down at the table next to me and started on his dinner.

"So, how has your afternoon been?" he asked between bites.

"Good," I replied. "I had a good talk with Mama today."

"How is she?"

"She's good. My goal is to get her out here for a visit." I slowly smiled. "What do you think? You think Roswell is big enough for two big-city girls?"

"Well, I don't know. The one who's already here is pretty much throwing us simple folk for a loop. We might need to get a little more prepared first."

I laughed and hit his arm playfully. "Honestly, I'm not that bad. Besides, I'm adapting." I stood. "I mean, look at me," I said, turning around for his inspection. "I'm wearing Wranglers and boots. Now you never could have convinced me a year ago that would happen."

He studied me quietly for a moment, allowing his gaze to roam over me. A sudden softness enter his gray eyes as he said, "You're wearing this life well."

I was instantly warmed, not only by the unexpected compliment, but by the look in his eyes as well. I couldn't remember the last time a man looked at me without lust or something close to it in his eyes. Hayden's eyes were sincere.

"Thank you," I finally said.

"You're welcome." He cleared his throat before returning to his dinner.

"I think I'll get her out here sooner or later," I said, charting my drifting thoughts back toward safer waters.

"I'm sure you will."

I let my gaze roam around the large kitchen again. "Have you never lived anywhere else?"

He finished his dinner and took the plate over to the sink. "Nope. I've never had a desire to. I travel every now and then for ranch business, but this is home."

I smiled. "I don't really blame you for not wanting to leave. It's beautiful here."

"It is," he agreed, his expression thoughtful.

We moved into the living room. I sat on the leather sofa and Hayden sat down next to me. He leaned back, stretching his long legs out in front of him and draped an arm across the back of the sofa.

"So, what made you decide to come here? I mean, there are plenty of places you could have started over. Why Roswell of all places?"

"You mean besides wanting to see aliens up close?"

He chuckled. "Yeah, besides that."

"Well, I guess I just wanted to completely start

over and get as far from Atlanta as I could. And when Caroline and David offered to let me stay with them I thought, why not? Roswell is as good a place as any, and at least I would be with friends. So, here I am."

Hayden smiled. "This is a good place to be." He ran a hand back through his hair. "To tell you the truth, I think I'd go out of my mind in the city. Too noisy and too much traffic. I guess I've always needed breathing room."

"I can understand that." I sighed. "Before coming here I couldn't have, but I do now."

He grinned. "So you really like it here, huh?"

"I do."

"I'm glad."

I stayed for another hour or so, soaking up amusing conversation with Hayden. We could talk about absolutely nothing and still wind up laughing about something. I loved that he could always make me laugh, even when I didn't feel like it. He had a way about him that made me feel so comfortable, it was like we had known each other for years.

The sun had gone down and the sky was dark when I finally said goodnight and headed back to the main house.

"Sorry I was so long with the truck," I said to David as I entered the kitchen. He and Caroline were at the table having a piece of apple pie.

"Oh, that's all right, darlin'. We weren't worried." He smiled at his wife. "Were we, honey?"

"Not at all," Caroline responded, smiling at me.

"Did you have a good visit?"

"I did." I took a glass from the cupboard and filled it with water, smiling as I lifted it to my lips. I had come to recognize Caroline and David's smiles and I was on to their matchmaking efforts. However, I decided to go on ignoring their subtle attempts. I would just pretend to remain oblivious, because when it came to contemplating another relationship, that's what I wanted now, to be oblivious.

"He got the leak fixed," I finally said.

"That's good," Caroline remarked. "It would have been awful if it had gotten any worse, especially with all the work he's already put into that house."

"I'm sure he feels the same." I finished my water and put the glass in the sink. Staring through the kitchen window for a moment, I watched the moths fluttering in and out of the light shining from the back porch. My gaze moved up to the curtains hanging over the window. "Are you still planning to wash some of the curtains tomorrow?"

"If I can get everything else done first."

"Why don't you let me take care of it for you?"

"Well, if you don't mind. It would sure be a big help to me." Caroline paused and grinned. "I always knew that height of yours was good for more than just modeling."

I laughed. "I guess so." I stretched and yawned, suddenly very tired. "I think I'll turn in early then. I'll see you both in the morning."

"All right, honey," Caroline said with a smile.

"Goodnight."

"Goodnight." I left them then, and headed to my room as my mind anticipated another tiring, yet productive morning to come.

I was tired, but I knew it was going to take a little time for me to wind down. I figured a little relaxing music would probably do the trick. I walked over to the dresser and grabbed my portable CD player and my case of CDs. Sitting on the bed, I flipped through the selection and tried to decide what I was in the mood for. My music taste ranged from Miles Davis, Nat King Cole, and Barbara Streisand, to Josh Groban, Keith Urban, and Brad Paisley. I just loved good music.

After a moment of contemplation, I pulled out a Nat King Cole CD and put it in the player. I skipped ahead to one of my favorite songs. *Unforgettable* has always relaxed me and made me smile. I put the headphones on, lay back against the pillows, and closed my eyes as the sultry sound of Nat's voice mellowed my thoughts.

As I began to softly hum along, my thoughts wandered back to my senior year in high school. Back then I had two good friends who were as close to me as sisters, and Nat King Cole was one of our favorite singers. He was before our time, but he was timeless, and still is. The three of us often got together for karaoke parties at Keisha's house and Nat's songs were usually the first ones we would perform to. We were quite the group; Keisha with her long micro braids, Rhonda with her relaxed locks, and me with a head full of long, barely tamable curls. We were so alike. We even shared the same skin coloring and our tastes in clothes were similar. And we *all* wanted to be models.

We were dubbed by our friends as the S.S.S.-the Singing Sister Society, because that's what we loved to do. We thought we would always be that close. We thought we would hang out together forever.

We had been wrong.

Rhonda never became a model. She became a drug addict instead. She died of an overdose at twenty, and I was devastated. Keisha modeled for a few years in Atlanta before experiencing a downward spiral with anorexia. Thankfully, she overcame it. She eventually married and moved to Florida. The last I had heard from her, she had just given birth to a little girl. That was three years ago. People say I was the successful one, but as far as I was concerned, it was Keisha who had truly succeeded. She had the love of a good man and she had her child. *That* was success. All I had was a full bank account and an empty heart. Older and a little wiser now, I would gladly trade one for the other.

As the last strains for *Unforgettable* filtered softly in my ears, I opened my eyes and stared at the ceiling, suddenly feeling very alone. The feeling was unwelcome and I had no desire to let it dwell.

I turned the player off and turned out the light.

"Tomorrow is a new day," I sighed as I pulled

the covers over me and closed my eyes. "Tomorrow is a new day."

I spent the next morning and part of the afternoon washing all the curtains and dusting around the windows. Caroline's home was actually filled with more country decor than southwestern. The curtains were floral, gingham, and lace. All the beds in the house were covered with country quilts and the tables were draped in handmade lace. Each and every room was cozy and inviting. The whole home was definitely Caroline and David.

As I stood on a chair in the kitchen to hang a pair of freshly washed curtains, my thoughts strayed to Hayden's home. *It* was definitely *him*, rugged yet beautiful. The colors in his home were neutral, which gave it a masculine feel without being overly so. The contrast in the two homes was stark, but they were equally beautiful.

I leaned over the sink a little more, trying to snap the curtain rod in place. The window was set pretty high. My arms and legs were long, but at the moment I was really stretching them to the limit. I almost had the rod snapped in when I felt the chair begin to tip and I gasped. Just as I was preparing for a painful fall, two large hands circled my waist and steadied me, accompanied by the deep voice that had become as familiar to me as my own name.

"Careful, darlin'. Can't have you breaking that pretty little neck of yours."

I turned and looked over my shoulder to see Hayden smiling up at me. I took a deep breath and smiled back. My heart was still racing, but not from losing my balance. "Good thing you were here. A moment later and you would have found me sprawled on the floor in pain."

"Let me help you down." His hands tightened on my waist a little, almost fully encircling it.

I put my hands on his massive shoulders, feeling the hard muscles beneath his shirt and felt instant heat rise to my face. I shook my head slightly and stepped down from the chair.

"You all right?" he asked, releasing me.

"I'm fine, just a little clumsy today."

"I could stay in here and spot you while you put the rest up if you'd like." His voice was teasing, but surprisingly, his eyes weren't.

"I'll be fine," I assured him. "You just go on about your manly duties."

He chuckled. "Manly duties, huh?"

"Yeah, you know, cowboy stuff."

"Cowboy stuff?" he repeated with a grin.

"Yeah. Riding, roping, wrangling. That stuff."

He laughed. "Well, I'll tell ya, if that's all there was to ranching, I'd be a boring old soul. But don't you worry none. I'll make sure I take care of my manly duties, starting with keeping you safe from bodily harm, all right?"

"All right," I agreed with a chuckle.

"I'll come back and check on you in a few."

"Well, knowing you'll be around will make me feel a lot safer."

He smiled and went to look for David. I watched him as he left the kitchen and couldn't help chuckling to myself again. He had brightened my already bright morning without even trying. Truthfully, he never had to try, he just did. That thought stayed with me through the rest of the day.

A laugh is as soothing as stargazing. And love can be as subtle as a runaway freight train.

Seven

As the weeks continued to pass, I found myself feeling more and more content with life. I took Caroline's advice and tried to familiarize myself with every aspect of ranching. I even got to know the ranch hands better and occasionally spent time casually observing them in their work. From helping them feed the cattle and horses to watching an injured animal being doctored, it was all interesting to me. I almost felt like a kid being let loose for the first time in an amusement park, anxious to take in everything I could.

There were a few times when Chris, one of the younger ranch hands, even asked me if I wanted to help him in the barn with one thing or another. I always said yes, but I was never with him for very long because Hayden usually came in and told me he or Caroline needed me for something else. After the third time, Chris stopped asking, which didn't bother me too much. He talked and stared more than he worked anyway. It was kind of sweet in a way.

But the most exciting thing for me to do around the ranch was watch Hayden break horses. It was a little frightening sometimes and I feared for him, but I always reminded myself that he knew what he was doing. He told me he loved having me around because it made him feel like he was doing something important, and he joked that he was going to make a cowgirl out of me yet.

Thinking about that always made me smile. Living life on a ranch was never on my list of dreams and aspirations. Of course, marrying an unfaithful man and being divorced at twenty-six wasn't a part of my plans either, but this was my life now. And as crazy as it might seem to some people, I loved it, and I was okay with it.

I grew to absolutely love horses and went riding whenever possible. I loved the feeling of freedom that came whenever I went riding. Every now and then Hayden would even join me.

On one particular afternoon Hayden got his work finished early, saddled a horse, and headed out with me. We rode for a while, then we stopped and talk while the horses rested. Hayden said he was impressed that I had taken to riding so quickly. I told him I went riding a couple of times when I was thirteen. A woman my mother worked for at that time invited us to her home one summer afternoon for lunch. Her fifteen year old son took me riding and I really liked it.

We sat underneath a large tree and Hayden flashed a teasing grin. "So, was it just the riding that was so much fun or the boy who took you?"

I grinned slyly. "Both actually."

He took off his hat and leaned back against the tree, stretching out his long legs. I casually let my eyes roam the length of him. He had no idea just how incredible he was, and I had no doubt he'd broken a lot of hearts without even realizing it.

"So," he said, causing me to rein in my thoughts, for which I was extremely grateful. "Tell me about this boy you went gallivanting off with."

"He was actually pretty cute. He had blond hair and blue eyes. He was nice, and very talkative."

"I'll bet he was," Hayden said with a chuckle.

I sighed. "I've never told anyone this, but . . . I received my first kiss that day."

His brows rose in surprise. "You're joking!"

"Nope. It wasn't that we really liked each other that much. I think it was more out of curiosity. I wanted to know what it was like. I knew he had kissed other girls before me, but I was the first *black* girl he'd ever kissed." I chuckled. "I'm sure he bragged about it to his friends once school started again. As for me, I never intended to tell anyone. And I never have, until now."

"Why didn't you tell anybody?" he asked, staring at me curiously.

"Well, partly because I didn't think my friends

would take it very well. Kissing a white boy just wasn't done. And I guess I wanted to forget about it because it didn't mean anything. After that, I promised myself that I would never kiss anyone again until it meant something."

He smiled. "Well, how was it for a first kiss?"

"It wasn't worth giving my kiss away so soon. No shooting stars. No butterflies, just wet."

Hayden laughed and I couldn't help laughing too. It had been a dumb thing to do, but it was pretty funny now. He stood and helped me up, and we mounted the horses again.

"You won't tell anyone my secret will you?" I asked, feigning concern.

Putting his hat back on, he grinned and winked. "I promise, darlin', your secret is safe with me. And if it will make you feel any better, I'll share a secret with you."

"Really?" I said, arching an eyebrow. "Do tell."

He moved his horse closer and said, "I didn't kiss a girl until I was nineteen."

"You're kidding!" Now it was my turn to be surprised.

"I'm not. I was scared to death of girls when I was a teenager. Took me a long time to get up the courage to kiss a girl."

Against my will, my eyes traveled to his lips, and with a good deal of effort I managed to keep my gaze from lingering. When the corner of his mouth twitched slightly I knew he had noticed my slip. I cleared my throat. "I would never have guessed you were afraid of girls," I finally said.

"Well, good." He adjusted his hat. "And by the way, you're the only person I've ever told, so just keep that little tidbit to yourself."

I grinned. "Don't worry. Your secret is safe with me."

I came to picture myself growing old in Roswell. I found that I had no desire to leave. And now that I was actually putting down some roots, I decided that I needed my own transportation. One afternoon Hayden took me to a couple of car lots in town, and after an hour or two of indecision, I decided on a new, pearl-colored *Cadillac Escalade*. It was pretty yet practical and pampering. Hayden said it was me. I took that as another compliment.

Now that I had my own transportation, I felt a little more independent. Not that I really had to worry that much about getting around. David's truck was available to me most of the time and Hayden was always happy to take me anywhere I needed to go, which was mainly to the store every now and then for personal items. Most of the time, I didn't even have to ask because he usually stopped by the house on his way into town and asked me if I wanted to ride in with him. I truly enjoyed those rides. I enjoyed being with him, period.

Whenever I thought about that fact, I felt both unsettled and confused, so I tried *not* to think about it. I couldn't let myself, because that train of thought would lead to no good. I knew it would. For now, I would not let myself go there.

Despite the size of the town, I was never bored. With Hayden's help, I always found ways to stay amused.

On one particular evening after the sky had darkened, I decided to go for a drive. Hayden and I jumped into my SUV and drove to the nearest convenience store for a couple of drinks. Then we opened the sunroof, rolled down the front windows, and cruised out into the desert and parked. There was no moon that night, but the stars twinkled brightly in the pitch black sky.

I reclined my seat back slightly and sighed. "The stars were never this bright in the city."

Hayden made an agreeing noise and leaned back also. "The desert is dry and barren during the day, but the view at night can't be topped."

I smiled. "Kind of makes me wish I owned a telescope."

He turned to me and I saw his grin through the darkness. "You wanna star gaze, or look for some of them little green men hovering around?"

"Why star gaze, of course. However, should a flying saucer happen to appear, I'll simply pull out your roll of aluminum foil and I'll be protected."

Hayden chuckled. "Well, that may stop them

from reading your thoughts, sugar, but what about abduction?"

"You'll protect me, won't you?" I asked, feigning concern.

"Don't worry, darlin'," he said, reaching over and brushing a lock of curls back from my face. He sighed and added in a simpering drawl, "I would give my life before I let them beam you up in one of them ships and start experimenting on you and then send you back down here pregnant with one of them alien babies."

I laughed out loud. "Thank you for being willing to protect my honor and keep me safe from alien breeding."

"No problem," he said with a chuckle.

I stared at his shadowed profile for a moment as he tipped his head back again. *Why does his voice always sound so alluring?* I wondered. *And in the darkness it's even more so.* I closed my eyes and shook my head slightly. *Don't go there, girl. Don't think.*

I tried to keep my thoughts in check, but I couldn't seem to change the course they were traveling. Maybe it was because I was sitting next to him shrouded in darkness. Maybe it was the ambiance of the twinkling stars above us or the soothing desert silence that caused my mind to run rampant into areas best left untouched. But one thing was certain. It was becoming harder and harder to ignore the feelings stirring inside me.

I leaned back again and looked up through the

sunroof. "You know, it's hard to believe you've never been married."

"I was," Hayden drawled suddenly.

I looked at him, startled. "What?"

"Yeah, I had a wife, but . . . she was . . . she was abducted." A chuckle suddenly rumbled from deep in his chest.

"Hayden!" I cried, shoving him.

He caught my hand. "I'm sorry, darlin', but I just couldn't resist."

"Now I know why you've never been married. You are impossible!"

"You're right about that," he agreed with mirth.

I laughed. When he said nothing more, I said, "You're avoiding an answer, aren't you?"

He instantly sobered and I almost felt like apologizing. I was about to when he finally said, "I guess I've always been married to the land."

"And why is that?" I asked softly.

He sighed. "Well . . . because I know the land will always be here." He leaned back again and became silent.

Okay, Mr. Cryptic, what does that mean? His silence left me full of questions, but I didn't ask them. I knew there had to be more to his answer though, and I suddenly found myself longing to know his every thought.

Don't go there, girl, I admonished myself for the fiftieth time today. *Just enjoy the evening.* I took a deep breath, vowing that I would do just that. And I did.

The next week I found a long wrapped box in my vehicle. I opened it, happiness rushing through me as my eyes fell on the new *Galileo* telescope. It was one of the most touching and thoughtful gifts I had ever received. I immediately went to find Hayden and thanked him.

"You're welcome," he said with a smile. "Tell you what. Let's head back out tonight and try that thing out."

"Okay," I said, my smile wide. "Drinks are on me tonight."

And that night we drove back out into the desert and gazed at the stars.

When I finally got in bed that night, I drifted to sleep thinking I'd never had a more enjoyable evening.

I was in Caroline and David's home for two months when I truly began to accept my growing feelings for Hayden. And that acceptance didn't come subtly. It hit hard and fast. I knew my feelings for him were strong, but I didn't realize just how strong and deep they went until the day there was an unexpected visitor at the ranch.

Hayden pulled his truck up in back of the house. We had just come back from picking up some things at the store for Caroline.

"Hey, Hayden," Tom, one of the hands called as he exited the kitchen door with a gallon container of iced tea. "You got a visitor. Been here about twenty minutes or so." He grinned and turned toward the bunkhouse.

I was wondering about Tom's silly grin when Hayden said, "Must be important if they're still here."

We grabbed the bags from the back of the truck. "You sure we remembered everything?" he asked as we headed up to the door.

"I sure hope so. You know Caroline. If we didn't, she'll send us right back to the store."

"You're right about that."

"Of course, it would give me another opportunity to toss oranges at you."

He chuckled. "No way, darlin'. I've had about all I can take today. But just remember, payback is gonna be sweet."

I laughed, thinking about how much fun it had been going shopping with him. Spending time with Hayden had now become the highlight of each day for me.

We were still discussing our produce escapades as we entered the kitchen and placed the bags on the counter.

"Well, hey, Hayden." The laugh-filled voice startled us both. We turned, noticing for the first time the woman sitting at the table with Caroline, who, at the moment had a strained look on her face.

"Hey, Debra," Hayden said with a grin. "What brings you out here?"

"I came out here to see you, of course. I know I'm twenty miles away, but you've been MIA for a while now. What have you been up to?"

He pushed his hat back a little and scratched his head. "Been busy," was all he said.

Feeling more than a little uncomfortable with the tanned blond present, I turned to start putting the groceries away when Caroline stood and moved to stand by me. The blatantly annoyed look she gave Hayden was definitely not missed by either of us. She smiled, placing her hand on my arm. "Debra, this is my friend, Raine. Raine, this is Debra Carson. She lives up the road a piece. I got to know her mother well before she passed away."

"It's good to meet you," I said, looking down at the voluptuous woman.

"Good to meet you, too," she said back.

I watched her eyes roam over me briefly, then instantly dismiss me. She casually adjusted her low cut blouse making it even lower.

Now that was a floozy move if I ever saw one. My eyes narrowed as she stood and moved closer to Hayden.

"So, what are your plans today, handsome?" She smiled, slipping an arm around his waist.

Her words were like a stab to my heart, causing a pain I had never experienced before. Before Hayden could answer, I said, "I'm going to see if Tom needs any help in the stable." I quickly turned and left.

Against The Odds

Words are faulty, unless it's the heart that is doing the talking.

Eight

Walking toward the horse stable, I blinked back the tears stinging my eyes. I kept asking myself how I could let my emotions get away from me this way. How had this happened? I thought I was being strong. I had fought so hard against these feelings because I hadn't wanted them, but they had persisted, tying my insides up in knots. And truthfully, I was beyond fighting them now.

I walked into the stable and found Tom pitching some fresh straw into one of the stalls.

"Need any help?" I asked, keeping my voice level and emotion-free.

He looked up at me with surprised eyes and smiled. "No, I think I got it covered."

I fell quiet for a minute, not really knowing what to do with myself. I wasn't about to go back into the house. Not if I could help it. "Are you sure?" I finally asked again.

Tom looked at me again and I saw a trace of sympathy in his eyes.

"Tell you what. Why don't you do these last few stalls for me while I go and help David with some things."

I smiled, relieved. "Thank you."

"No problem." He handed me the pitchfork and left.

Left alone with my thoughts, I stabbed at the bale, loosening more straw, and tossed it into the stall Tom had been working on. I figured tossing straw in was a lot better than having to muck the stalls out. I continued to work, doing my best to keep my thoughts away from Caroline's kitchen where Hayden was, with Debra, the 'Blond cowgirl.' I tried, but I couldn't keep myself from agonizing over who the woman was to Hayden.

It was obvious from the way Debra looked at Hayden that there had been something between them. At least it seemed that way. And what about Hayden's reaction to seeing her? He hadn't even thought to introduce us. Caroline finally had to do it. It was almost as if I wasn't there, like I had suddenly turned invisible or something.

I heaved a frustrated sigh. I knew I had no right to be upset with Hayden. No reason at all. He had been a good friend to me and he was free to spend time with whoever he wanted to. There was nothing between us, and though I had feelings for him, I doubted that he felt anything other than friendship for me. That thought, most of all hurt deeply.

I sighed again. He was an incredible man, too beautiful and too perfect for words. And I knew I would never be more to him than I already was. I would just have to be all right with that. Maybe this was to be my lot in life. Maybe all I would ever be to any man worth having was a friend. If that was all I could ever be to Hayden, then I would have to deal with it. This is what I told myself, but it did nothing to quell the ache I carried inside.

I was so lost in my thoughts, I didn't even hear Hayden approach.

"You keep forking that straw in there like that, there ain't gonna be room for the horse." He smiled and popped a strawberry into his mouth. I figured he must have taken it from the container we bought for Caroline. His shirt was now unbuttoned and hanging open, exposing the hard muscles of his tanned chest and torso.

I looked at the stall and paused in my work, chagrined as I realized I had practically pitched two whole bales of straw into the one stall. I chuckled. "I'll bet Tom will never let me do this again." I felt myself sober a bit, but I quickly smiled again and turned away, not wanting him to see the pain in my eyes. Nor did I want him to see how just being near him now affected me. I was beginning to think about things I hadn't fully allowed myself to. Things like how it would feel to have his massive arms around me, the smell and feel of his skin, and the sensation and taste of his kiss. I had never had these kinds of thoughts before, not even about Jerome. And I had married him!

Shake it off, girl! I shook my head slightly, attempting dislodge the painful thoughts and began removing some of the straw from the stall.

"No, leave it," he said playfully, taking the pitchfork from my hands. "At least the horse will be comfy."

I smiled. "Stop making fun of me," I said, shoving him.

He suddenly got that mischievous look in his eyes I knew so well. "Shove me again, woman and you'll be wearing that straw."

"Are you threatening me?" I asked, shoving him again.

"All right now. You're asking for it."

Just as I was about to shove him a third time, his large hands shot out and grabbed my waist. I laughed and struggled to get away, but it was a futile attempt. He pick me up and slung me over his shoulder like a sack of potatoes and entered the stall.

"Hayden McKade, don't you dare!" I yelled.

"Why not? Don't you wanna try out this straw? It's nice and fresh."

"No, I don't. Put me down or so help me I'll . . ." I didn't get a chance to say more because the next thing I knew, he knelt and dropped me in the straw.

"I can't believe you!" I said, laughing.

"Well, you told me to put you down," he said, smiling down at me. "So I did."

"You know I'll get you back for this," I said, gripping the front of his shirt in my hands.

"I know." His voice turned surprisingly raspy. He quickly sobered, his expression changing as he looked into my eyes.

As I lay there looking up at him, my heart began to beat wildly, almost hammering through my chest. Something was happening. I could feel it. We continued to wordlessly stare at one another when his gaze moved to my mouth. My breathing became shallow as he placed his hands on either side of me in the straw. He slowly lowered himself against me and teased the corner of my mouth with a light kiss. I released a breathy sigh and my lips parted slightly. When that happened his whole mouth descended upon mine in an instantly heated exchange.

A soft moan escaped me, coming from deep inside as his moist mouth claimed mine, his lips caressing mine, plying them with burning affection. He pulled me tighter against him, so tight that I could feel his heart beating madly. The sweep of his tongue over mine was utterly sensual and his mouth tasted sweet, like the strawberry he'd eaten. I wrapped my arms around his neck, pressing a hand into his thick hair. His beard was prickly against my skin as he continued to administer his driven kisses, but I loved it. I loved *him*. Deep down I think I had loved him from day one.

After another moment, his kiss softened. He

made a pleasurable noise as his lips lightly toyed with mine. Then he buried his hand in my hair, gently tugged my head back slightly, and pressed a warm lingering kiss in the hollow of my neck, making me shudder.

"You smell so good," he whispered. He pulled back slightly. "And you taste just like I thought you would."

"And how is that?" I whispered back.

"Like warm honey," he growled against my mouth. He finally rolled on to his back and pulled me against him. I rested my head against his chest. He took my hand and pressed it against his lips, and the feel of his mouth again sent shivers of pleasure through me.

"You don't know how long I've wanted to be with you like this," he said, breaking the silence. His voice was even raspier and his breath was hot on my skin.

"How long?" I breathed, not able to believe I was with him this way, and that he was saying these things to me.

Instead of answering, he released my hand and lifted my chin, urging me to look at him. After a moment, he said, "There's nothing going on with me and Debra." When I said nothing, he went on. "She's a fun girl and we used to have a lot of laughs, but that's all there was to it. She's nothing more than a friend. I made that clear to her today, so I doubt she'll be coming back this way for a while."

I raised up and leaned into him, pressing my

hand over his beard, pausing to run a finger across his lips. "Then what am I?" I asked, feeling tingly all over.

He tightened his arms around me, staring into my eyes. "You're the woman who has had my heart twisting in the wind from the moment I met you." He smiled, caressing my back with his long fingers. "When we went to Dale's that day and you managed to charm *him*, a crusty old farmer, that was it for me. If I knew nothing else that day, I knew I wanted you to be mine."

I smiled widely, not able to believe he'd really felt that way. "But why haven't you said anything before now?"

He pushed a hand back through his chestnut locks and sighed, staring up at the stable roof for a moment. "I don't know. Truthfully, I think I was scared. I was scared of scaring you. I mean, it had only been six months or so since your marriage ended and I figured you'd want to stay as far away from another relationship as possible. Besides," he added with a smile, "I'm just a sweaty old cowboy."

I sighed, raising up. He pulled me on top of him and I looked down into his eyes, smiling. "Sweaty is good. It means you're a hard worker. You're not soft. And you're right, I didn't want to get involved with anyone. I wasn't ready. But to be honest, my marriage was over long before the divorce. When I married Jerome, I wasn't in love. It was a purely shallow decision. He was successful, a very desired bachelor and he gave me attention. I eventually grew to care for him very much, but it was never truly like it should have been. Mama had raised me to be an old fashioned girl. She told me I needed to save myself for the person I intended to marry. Sadly, I didn't take her advice. I let my head be turned and my morals be altered." I paused, looking into his eyes intently. "I have enough respect for myself now that I won't let that happen again."

He moved his hand from my back and buried it in my hair once more, crushing the curls in his fingers. "I'm glad." He smiled, causing me to melt inside like butter in a hot skillet. Then his expression turned serious. "If I just wanted someone to warm my bed, I could get that from Debra with no problem. I mean, I'm not completely innocent where women are concerned, but I ain't a rambler either."

Try as I might, I couldn't stop myself from asking, "Have you . . . have you ever been with her in that way? I mean, I know you said there was never anything serious between you two, but . . . sometimes that doesn't matter."

When he didn't answer, I averted my eyes and started to pull back a little, wishing I had never asked him. That was his business. I was about to tell him just that when he touched a finger to my lips and held me against him.

"Look at me, baby," he finally said, and I bravely raised my eyes to his. "I didn't say there was never anything serious between us. I said there was never anything between us, period. That's not what I wanted."

I smiled then. "So, what *do* you want?"

He tightened his arm around my waist possessively. "I want you, darlin'. In the worst way."

"I'm glad, because I want you too." I sighed softly and rested my head against his solid chest, feeling heat radiating from his skin.

"I always wanted you for mine, Raine. And I gotta tell you, it pretty near drove me insane to see Chris gawking at you the way he was. I figured I had best nip that in the bud real quick."

I raised up and grinned. "I wondered why he stopped asking me to help him. I guess you were making your claim even then, huh?"

"Dang straight I was. And when I came in the stable that last time and he had his arms on either side of you supposedly showing you how to bridle a horse, I damn near flew apart." When I chuckled, he said, "You laugh all you want, sugar, but I was pretty near ready to rope that boy up by his boots."

Snorting, I tried to stifle a laugh, but I couldn't. As soon as the mental picture of poor Chris hanging upside down by his boots with Hayden holding the end of the rope entered my mind, I lay back in the straw and roared with laughter. Hayden started laughing as well.

I finally got a hold of myself and wiped my eyes. Turning to him, I pressed a hand to his face, caressing his beard. "You never had anything to worry about. Though I wasn't willing to admit it to myself, I was yours even then. There's not another man in this world like you, Hayden McKade."

"And there ain't another woman like you."

I smiled, still not able to believe this was happening, that he actually felt more for me than friendship. To be with him this way was amazing, and more wonderful than I ever dreamed. I pressed my face against his chest. "Well, at least I know there's nothing wrong with me now."

"Now why would you think there was something wrong with you?"

For the first time since the divorce, I opened my mind and seriously pondered that question, and I was amazed to have the answer come so quickly. "I guess after giving and giving in my marriage just so Jerome could keep cheating, I started doubting myself. I started to feel like I wasn't good enough. I thought once the divorce was final I would be over it, but every now and then the feeling comes back."

He released a sigh and I heard the slight sadness in his next words. "And I guess my not letting you know how I felt about you didn't help matters." When I said nothing, he gently took my chin in his hand, urging me to look at him. "Let me tell you something, Raine. There ain't a thing wrong with you. It sounds like that mule's hind end you married had the problem. He didn't know what he had when he had you. And if he really loved you, he wouldn't have been chasing behind some other skirt." He caressed my face. "I promise I will never hurt you, Raine. You're a beautiful and incredible woman, and you're more than enough woman for me."

I grinned and raised up to kiss him again. He rolled and turned me onto my back. Then his mouth descended upon mine with a heat that I felt all over. I literally saw stars and I felt a tidal wave of emotion washing over my entire being. His kisses were completely rapturous. They left me breathless and completely filled at the same time.

"I can't get enough of you, baby," he whispered against my mouth. "Which is why," he added, suddenly sitting up and pulling me up with him, "we had better get out of here before we get into some serious trouble." He grinned and began picking straw from my hair. I was sure it would be an all day job. "After all," he continued, "a man can only be so strong, and when it comes to you, I can see now that my defenses are shot all to hell. I have no resistance whatsoever."

I smiled warmly, taking the front of his shirt in my hands. "I feel the same about you."

He sat staring at me for a moment and pressed a gentle hand to my cheek, brushing a thumb across my lips. I silently met his adamant gaze with my own and wondered what he was thinking. He quickly pulled me to him for one more hot, enrapturing kiss that I wanted to go on and on. Growling softly, he abruptly parted his lips from mine and stood, pulling me up.

"We have *got* to get out of here," he said with a grin. Grinning back, I drew his head down, not able to resist kissing him once more. Lacing my fingers through his, we left the stable and headed up to the house.

As we entered the kitchen, Caroline looked up and grinned in surprise. I knew we must have looked a sight. I was about to explain when she said, "My, my. It looks like you two had a nice roll in the hay."

My mouth immediately dropped open and she released a loud laugh. Hayden chuckled and came to my defense.

"You're a bad girl," he said to his smiling sister-in-law as he wrapped his arms around me and pressed me back against him. "Now you know Raine here ain't that kind of girl."

"Glad to hear it," she said, winking at me, her eyes twinkling with pleasure.

"Well," Hayden said as he released me, "I guess I had better get out there and get some work done." He looked down at me. "You wanna walk me back down?"

"Sure," I said, smiling up into his handsome face.

"She'll be back later." He took my hand in his.

We both chuckled when we heard Caroline's laughed filled voice call after us, "You two just make sure and stay away from the horse stable!"

Oh, the joy of new love!

Nine

During the next couple of weeks, Hayden and I stayed pretty busy around the ranch during the day. With summer officially here and new calves and colts to keep up with, there was always something to do. Even still, one of us usually managed to get away from our work for a few minutes to see the other. Occasionally, we even managed to sneak away for a few moments to be alone. Now that we were officially together, we couldn't seem to stay away from each other. And we were frequently kidded by Tom and the other hands. They jokingly accused us of slacking on the job.

Once when I was out walking, Hayden emerged from the barn and quickly pulled me in and shut the door. He pinned me against the wall, and for five minutes we practically devoured each other. There was so much heat generated between us, I'm surprised the barn didn't go up in flames. When we finally came back out, Ted was standing by the door waiting with a big grin on his face. He said he didn't want to interrupt, so he waited. Normally, I would have been completely embarrassed, but as I looked up into Hayden's eyes and saw the emotion burning in them as he gazed at me, I wasn't embarrassed a bit.

I lived for breakfast, lunch, and dinner time, but not because of hunger. I usually sat staring at Hayden more than I ate, which he finally commented on one day by saying, "I told you darlin', if you're not careful, you're gonna disappear." I laughed and forced myself to finish my meal. But I did tell him it was definitely his fault that I didn't feel like eating. He quickly kissed me and told me he was sorry.

Never in my life had I ever felt so emotionally connected to someone. I couldn't even be near Hayden without touching him, without having him touch me. He was on my mind almost every minute of the day. I missed him when he worked and he told me he ached to be with me as well. So, I went from one moment to the next, anticipating the time when I would finally get to be with him again.

And so went our days. But our evenings were spent in each other's arms. I loved evenings.

On one particular day, Hayden had been out all

day on another part of the property repairing some fence lines. When he made his rounds to check the animals that morning, he found that a couple of cows had gotten out. After bringing them in, stitching up a few cuts, and administering antibiotic shots, he went back out. So I didn't get to see him at breakfast. He hadn't even come back for lunch, and I missed him terribly.

When he finally came through the door for dinner, I was so happy to see him, I immediately ran to him and jumped into his arms. He lifted me up off the floor, holding me against him. He was dirty and sweaty, but I didn't care. I was with him again and nothing else mattered.

He pulled back a little and pressed a salty kiss to my lips. "Missed me, huh?" he said, a tired grin on his face.

"Missed you is an understatement," Caroline said as she set another plate on the table.

"Well, I was having some Raine withdrawals myself," he said, kissing me again.

Caroline grinned. "Oh, I think we are way past withdrawals here."

"Poor thing didn't know what to do with herself," David added with a wide smile.

"All right, you two. I haven't been that bad," I shot back with feigned annoyance.

"Whatever you say, darlin'," David said, trying to keep a straight face.

Hayden chuckled. "Well, if you two don't

mind," he drawled, grinning down at me, "I think I'll take my dinner back to the house. I'm starving." He glanced at the table and added, "Oh, and I'll take some food, too."

David hooted out loud and I softly punched Hayden. He just laughed and kissed me.

"Did you get the fence fixed?" Dave asked Hayden as I moved to the table and dished up a couple of plates of food for us.

"For the most part. It'll hold for the time being."

Caroline took a wooden tray from the bottom cupboard and I placed the plastic covered plates on it, along with a couple of pieces of pie.

I could feel Hayden's gaze following me as I moved around the kitchen, and the look in his eyes warmed me almost as much as his touch. Indeed, his look at that moment *was* like a touch. He had no idea how much his very presence affected me. Then again, maybe he did. I met his adoring gaze with my own and determined that there was enough electricity between us to light up the whole state of New Mexico.

I held the tray on my lap in the truck as Hayden drove to his place. As soon as we got in the house I took the food to the kitchen and reheated it while he took a quick shower. Ten minutes later, he entered the kitchen wearing clean jeans, no shirt, and barefoot. Just seeing him this way did heady things to my emotions.

"Come here, baby," he said in that low drawl of his.

I immediately stood and went into his warm

embrace. Standing on my tip-toes, I pressed my face against his neck and breathed in the intoxicating and familiar scent of him. Tangling my fingers in his damp hair, I sighed.

"I missed you, Raine," he breathed, burying his face in my hair. He pulled back a little and looked down at me, his sensuous mouth curving up in a smile. "Let's hurry and eat." He pressed a work-roughened hand to my face, caressing it softly. "I've got some plans for you."

"Oh, really?" I comically arched an eyebrow, making him laugh. "Then by all means, let's hurry."

Hayden and I sat snuggled together on the porch swing with a quilt wrapped around us. A couple of mugs of hot chocolate sat on a white iron table. A large citronella candle burned brightly on another table. The night was cool, the sky was dark, and the stars were out. It was beautiful.

We quietly listened to the peaceful sounds that filled the night. A slight breeze rustled the leaves on the tall trees and the soft serenade of the crickets was soothing to our ears. The light of the full moon made the small grove of trees look magical, providing the perfect ambiance for us.

I pressed my head against Hayden's shoulder and he rested his chin against my forehead. As I sat with him this way, a feeling of warmth surrounded me that could not be put into words. In all my years of marriage to Jerome, I had never felt this kind of warmth. I never knew it existed, and I was happy to be making these new discoveries with Hayden.

The obvious differences between us would concern a lot of people if they were in our situation. Some people would be concerned about the whole black-white, cowboy-*city sister* thing. But these things didn't concern me, and they didn't concern Hayden. The differences meant nothing to either of us because they were shallow thoughts. However, *he* meant everything to me, *was* everything to me. In essence, I guess our differences are what drew us together. Now, he was the air that I breathed. And I knew at that moment, if I ever had to be away from him, my heart would literally break in two.

"Raine." Hayden's gentle voice drew me from my pondering. He lifted my chin and looked into my eyes, his gaze intent. He silently let his thumb caress my cheek for a moment. "I love you, baby." He smiled. "I love you so much, and I want you to be my wife."

The softly spoken words brought immediate tears to my eyes. I hadn't told him I loved him because he had never said the words to me. But oh, how I had wanted to tell him! How my soul had cried out the words! It cried out even now.

I pressed a hand to his bearded face as tears spilled down my cheeks, refusing to be stopped. "I love you, too," I whispered. "And being your wife is what I want more than anything."

He smiled, then took a ring box from his pocket. "Now I can give you this," he said, opening it and slipping the solitaire on my finger. Brushing the tears from my face with his fingers, he tightened his embrace. "Let's make it soon, Raine. I'm tired of living alone."

I looked into his eyes and smiled. "And I'm tired of having to say goodbye to you every night. I barely get any sleep because I'm usually lying there thinking about you, wishing you were next to me."

"You get sleep," he countered, grinning back at me. "Shoot, sugar, all I'm ever able to do most of the time is lie there all night staring up in the dark because I can't get you off my mind."

"So, that's where the bloodshot eyes are coming from these days."

"Dang straight. But don't you know it's worth it?"

I caressed his lips. "It is for me too."

He silently let his eyes roam over my face for a moment and slowly bent his head, capturing my mouth with his, igniting a fire in me that burned from the inside out. When he kissed me, everything else went away. Nothing else existed, and I knew his kisses would always affect me that way.

"How soon?" he whispered against my mouth. He pulled back a little. "Next week works for me."

"Are you serious?"

"Completely."

"Next week?"

"Next week."

I grinned in surprise, warmed by the knowledge that he really wanted me, that I was really going to be his wife. "Well, then, I guess next week would be fine with me, too."

He smiled before kissing me once more, and I knew in that moment that no matter what path my life would take in the future, this is the one I would forever be grateful for, because it led me to Hayden.

I had no idea, however, as we clung to each other under the stars, that our love was about to be tested in ways I never expected.

Reality always keeps a heart in check.

Ten

I was about to head out to where Hayden was finishing the repairs on another section of the fence when my cell phone rang. Checking my reflection in the full-length mirror once more, I picked it up and was startled the see the number for the Zuri Agency displayed on the caller ID.

"Hello," I answered and grinned when I was greeted by the voice of my friend, Andrea.

Andrea was a secretary for the agency, and a darned good one too. I always told her they never paid her enough, and I had heard it said more than once around the office that she was indispensable. I had only spoken with her a couple of times since coming to Roswell. Both times she called me from her home. This time, however, she called from the office, which surprised me.

"How are you, girl?" she asked, her voice ringing with energetic excitement.

"I'm good. What are you up to today?"

"No good as usual," she answered and I laughed.

"Well, judging from the caller ID, you must have something important to tell me because you never call from the office."

"I know. If I made a personal call from this office, girl, they would probably garnish my wages and tell me I owed them for the trouble."

I laughed at her exaggeration. "You know, I keep telling you to get from behind that desk and start modeling. The money is a lot better."

"Yeah, right. Me, modeling? That will be the day."

She always gave me the same answer. "So, what's going on?" I finally asked.

"What's going on is one of our top clients wants you for an ad for their new winter cosmetic line. They want you to be the new face of their company, and to put it simply, the agency wants you back."

"Who's the client?" I asked curiously. When there was a sudden knock at the door, I put my hand over the phone and said, "Come in." Caroline opened the door and I put up a finger, indicating I would only be a moment.

"The client is Ebersole & Company."

"You're kidding me!" I breathed incredulously.

Ebersole was not just one of their top clients,

they were the cream of the crop! Only two other models at Zuri had jobs with Ebersole, and they were only fill-ins for when the company needed an extra body on the runway for their clothing line. For me to actually be requested by them was truly amazing. I couldn't count the number of girls who would kill to model for them. A permanent gig with Ebersole was truly a model's one way ticket to the top.

"They're talking seven figures, Raine," she continued. "And they want you yesterday."

I blew out a breath and sat down on the side of the bed. I noticed Caroline still standing in the doorway. I motioned for her to have a seat. She sat in a rocker by the side of the bed, a curious look in her eyes.

"Andrea," I finally said. "I can't just pick up and come back. I have a life here now."

"You can't seriously be thinking of passing up an opportunity like this," she said in disbelief. "A chance like this comes zero times in a lifetime."

You're telling me! I thought. A gig with Ebersole would have completely overshadowed my other modeling jobs. Shoot, I probably wouldn't have even had to take any other jobs.

"Zero times in a lifetime, Raine!" Andrea's voice blared through the phone again.

"I know," I agreed with a sigh.

After a moment of strained silence between us, Andrea softly said, "You've found someone, haven't you?"

I closed my eyes and pressed my thumb and

index fingers to my temples. "Yes."

"All right, ask yourself this. Is he worth blowing a contract this big? Is he really worth it?"

I smiled, not hesitating to answer. "He is, Andrea."

I heard her heave an exasperated sigh. "I don't believe this," she muttered and sighed again. "At least think about it, Raine. Just tell me you'll think about it and call me back, all right?"

"I will," I finally said. But truthfully, my mind was already made up. "I'll call you later."

When Andrea said goodbye, I could hear relief in her voice. I looked over at Caroline, who had been waiting patiently.

"Your old life calling you back?" she asked, her voice soft and full of understanding.

"It's calling . . . but I'm not going back."

She smiled. "It's tempting though."

"I suppose," I conceded, then paused and thought, *Who in their right mind wouldn't be tempted?* I finally said, "It was a glamorous life and I made a lot of money, but it's not me anymore." I smiled. "This is my life now, being right here, with Hayden."

Caroline reached for my hand. "You've completely changed that man's life, Raine. Now I have to tell you something, but I don't want you to mention it to Hayden, all right?"

"All right," I agreed, wondering what it could possibly be, especially since she didn't want me to tell Hayden.

"Oh, don't worry," she said, evidently reading my thoughts in my expression. "It's nothing bad. I just wanted let you know that Hayden called me late last night on my cell phone. He said he needed to talk."

"Really?"I stated, surprised, wondering what he needed to talk about. I figured it must have been something really important to call her cell, apparently wanting to avoid having me answer the phone.

"I think he called me because he needed to be reassured of something."

"Reassured of what?"

"He worries about you one day getting tired of this kind of life. And he thinks there might come a day that you'll end up regretting your decision to marry him and want to leave."

I stared at her incredulously. "Why would he even think that? I love him. There is no way I would ever leave him."

"I guess he's been alone for so long that handing his heart over so completely to someone has overwhelmed him a bit. But I assured him you would never leave and I think he's okay now."

I sighed. "You know, when I made the decision to leave that world behind, I did it because I knew there had to be something more out there for me." I paused and swallowed at the sudden emotion in my throat. "And there was. With Hayden I have all I could ever want. There's nothing shallow about him. He really loves me. I can hear it in his voice, and I can feel it every time he touches me or even looks at me. He has given me something I never thought I would have. He's given me true happiness. After having a taste of such happiness, there is no way I could ever leave him, no matter how flattering the offer. So, I guess I'll have to prove to him every day that my life will always be here with him. Because I'm not going anywhere."

"I know." Caroline again smiled, her eyes filling with moisture. "I'm so glad you came."

"So am I," I said, squeezing her hand. Then I stood. "And now, I'm heading out to see my husband-to-be."

Caroline grinned. "Only three more days."

"Oh, I know," I groaned with happy anticipation.

"Well, you go on out to him."

Squeezing her hand again, I leaned down and kissed her cheek before heading out the door.

Love is not bliss. It's productive work.

Eleven

I parked beside Hayden's truck and turned off the ignition. I could see him in the distance, bent over the fence and working intently. I sat for a moment and silently watched him. Though he was still a little distance away, I could still make out the hardened muscles on his shirtless form, his skin bronzed by the sun and glistening with sweat. I decided long ago that he must have an aversion to shirts, but I didn't mind one bit. He was indeed a beautiful man, the most beautiful man I had ever seen, and I could look at him all day and never tire.

As I continued to watch him work, thoughts of the call from Andrea slowly began to seep back into my mind. I still couldn't believe the offer that had been made. Ebersole & Company had wanted *me* to be the new face for their fall cosmetic line! *Me* of all people! I couldn't help wondering why the offer had to come now of all times. I mean, I had done well for myself in the modeling industry and had made good money. I had enough money saved to be secure for a long time. But this! A seven figure contract!

I closed my eyes and pressed my head against the steering wheel. Truthfully, it wasn't so much the money I thought about. With the very large settlement from the divorce, as well as what I'd accumulated modeling, I had more than enough. No, it wasn't the money. It was the position. With that job, *I* would have been in with the cream of the crop!

I sighed and shook my head. Six months ago I would have jumped at the chance. Even four months ago. Anything to make me feel more beautiful, more desired.

But I don't need that anymore, I thought with a smile. *I don't need the praises of the 'beautiful people' of the world to make me feel beautiful, or desired. I have all those things with one beautiful person. The only one that counts.*

My thoughts shifted to my conversation with Caroline about Hayden's fear of me leaving. I couldn't believe he felt that way. There was no way I would ever leave him. I couldn't. It hurt to even think about being away from him. I mean, good grief, I could barely get through a whole day without seeing him as it was. He had become my whole life, my whole world. And he would always be.

The ringing of my cell phone startled me from my thoughts. I hesitantly took it from my purse and looked at the caller ID.

"You have got to be kidding me," I muttered as I stared at Jerome's office number. "This is really all I need."

"Hello."

"What's up, girl?" came Jerome's irritating voice.

What's up? What do you mean what's up? I couldn't believe he was calling me. Sure, our marriage hadn't ended on the worst of terms, but we weren't on the best either. "What do you want, Jerome?" I was in no mood to be cordial.

"Can't I just call to say hello?"

"No."

He laughed. "That's cold." When I heaved an irritated sigh, he went on. "Well, I heard it through the grapevine you got offered some serious *bling* money by Ebersole."

"And just how did you come by that info?" I asked, angry at him for intruding in my life.

"You know me, Raine. I pay well to stay informed."

The familiar arrogance in his voice made me fume. "Listen, Jerome. We're not married anymore, so stay out of my business and keep to your own, all right?"

"But your business *is* my business."

"Not anymore it isn't."

"I'm always going to care about you, Raine. You know you've been offered the chance of a lifetime, so come on back here, girl and take care of business."

I sighed and closed my eyes, leaning my head back against the seat. "Did Andrea put you up to this?"

"No, but the walls of Zuri have ears and I pay for those ears."

I pressed my head in my hand. "Stay out of my life, Jerome. Don't call me again."

He chuckled. "Something tells me you've found something warm and new out there, and I don't mean the scenery either. You're changing up on me girl, aren't you? Taking a little jaunt on the light side, huh? Well, that's okay because it's all good."

"Get a life," I muttered, sick to death of his 'stick to your own kind' mentality.

He laughed. "Well, just remember, girl, vanilla ice-cream gets boring pretty quick. I give you a year before chocolate is calling your name. That vanilla craving will never last."

"You are seriously screwed up, Jerome."

"You know I've always been a betting man," he continued, "so here is my prediction. A hundred to one odds, Raine. A hundred to one odds that you'll soon miss the life and the people you left. You're too different from the people out there in that hick town. You're a high maintenance woman, and without the glamor and big-city conveniences, your life will definitely be miserable."

I had heard enough. "Goodbye, Jerome," I said abruptly and hung up.

The nerve of him! I pushed a hand back through my hair, closed my eyes, and took a deep breath. *Okay, no more phone calls. And no more of that life. Everything I need is right here. All I want is right here.*

I opened my eyes and looked up just as Hayden turned and saw me, and my heart immediately leaped with joy. As he tossed his gloves aside and began walking in my direction, all my other thoughts completely faded into oblivion. I immediately jumped out and ran to him. As soon I entered the haven of his strong, protective and loving arms, I felt like I had come home. I wrapped my arms around his neck and he lifted me off the ground. I couldn't stop the tears burning my eyes as I pressed my face against his neck and molded to him.

"I've missed you, baby," he breathed against my cheek.

With that softly spoken phrase, the tears came. I gently took his handsome face in my hands and looked into his eyes.

"Are you all right?" he asked, apparently puzzled by my tears.

I nodded, not able to speak at the moment, unable to express to him everything that was in my heart. I finally pressed my lips lightly to his. "I love you so much," I whispered.

He continued to hold me, his eyes roaming over my face. When more tears began to spill down my cheeks, he lowered his head and immediately wove a spell over me with a warm, driven kiss. A kiss that completely gave to me, sinking into my every sense and making me long for the day when I would be completely his.

When his mouth finally released mine, he smiled and said, "I love you, woman." He put me down, took off his hat, and wiped an arm across his forehead. Then he flashed that adorable grin of his. "I was about ready to come and get you, you know."

Forcing myself not to feel guilty about my reason for being late, namely the phone call from the agency, I grinned back. "Impatient today, aren't we?" I said playfully.

"Dang straight, woman. Ain't you learned yet that you don't keep a man in love waiting?"

"I'm sorry," I said, smiling coyly. "I promise I'll make it up to you."

"Yeah, you will," he agreed, slipping an arm around me as we walked back toward the fence. "Just as soon as you become Mrs. McKade."

I nudged him in the ribs and he laughed. I slipped my hand in the back pocket of his worn jeans as we walked. "So, how much longer?"

"Probably another hour, maybe less."

"Need any help?"

"The only way you can help me, darlin', is by just standing there and giving me something beautiful to look at from time to time."

I was speechless. He had no idea how deeply his words had affected me. I quickly brushed a sudden tear away, hoping he wouldn't notice, but he did.

"Hey," he said, stopping and taking my chin in his hand. "What is it?"

I quickly smiled. "Nothing. I'm just looking forward to being your wife."

"And I'm looking forward to being your husband," he drawled, pressing a quick kiss to my lips. He looked at me for another moment, and I could almost feel him trying to read my thoughts, like he knew there was something wrong, only he didn't know what.

"Come on," I said, brightening and shoved him. "Quit slacking on the job and get going."

"I'll show you who's slacking." I took off running, but with his long stride, I didn't even make it a couple of yards before he caught me. He quickly picked me up, slinging me over his shoulder.

"Put me down!" I yelled, laughing.

"I can't, darlin'. Not enough straw around here."

"You!" I growled and he chuckled. Oh, how I loved him!

Sometimes claiming a new life can be as painful as it was joyful leaving the old one behind.

Twelve

After Hayden went home and showered and changed, we packed a picnic dinner, hopped into his truck, and headed to *Lea Lake* at the *Bottomless Lakes State Park*. The first time Hayden took me there, I completely fell in love with the place, so we went back as often as we could. *Lea Lake* was my favorite of the lakes because the water was crystal clear. I always imagined a whole enchanted underworld when I gazed into its depths. A world of mermaids and water nymphs with flowing hair spilling behind them as they swam through magical crevices, over mountainous crests, and through glittering stone arches. I could sit by the water for hours and let my imagination carry me away. It truly was a beautiful lake.

Hayden had told me the lakes weren't really bottomless. They just looked that way because of the greenish blue color that came from algae and other plants at the bottom. He said the lakes really were no more than ninety feet deep. I told him that to me, especially since I couldn't swim well, that *was* bottomless. In any case, I was anxious to be there again with him.

I sat in the middle of the seat close to Hayden as we enjoyed the scenic drive. We filled the time with talk of our wedding and everything we still needed to do to get ready.

"So, when is your mama flying in?"

"Friday at two in the afternoon, which gives me a day to help get her room ready at Caroline's."

He squeezed my hand and pressed it to his lips. "You pretty excited to see her?"

"I am." I couldn't help smiling as I thought of Mama's reaction to my announcement that I was getting married again. She didn't lecture me or drill me with a thousand questions. She only asked three. Did I love Hayden? Did he love me? Would he make me happy? I answered yes to all three, and that was that.

"Well, at least you'll reach your goal of getting her out here."

"That's true. And all I had to do is get engaged."

"Is that all?" he said, putting his arm around me.

I leaned over and pressed a kiss to his cheek. "I can't think of a better reason."

"Neither can I. But I *can* think of a better announcement, only we have to get married before we can make that happen."

I smiled, instantly warmed. "I look forward to having your babies, Hayden."

"They'll be beautiful, that's for sure."

Nodding, I pressed my head against his shoulder and thought about how much I longed to be the mother of his children. I had always wanted children, but the intense and deep love I felt for Hayden made my desire to be a mother even greater. I had no doubt he would be a wonderful father. I sighed deeply and let my thoughts continue as we settled into a comfortable silence.

After a few moments, my cell phone rang. I reached into my purse and mentally swore when the agency's number appeared on the ID screen. To say I was hesitant to answer was an understatement.

"You gonna answer that?" Hayden asked when it rang a third time.

I did my best to smile nonchalantly and pressed the button. My voice sounded strained when I answered, despite my best efforts.

"Sorry to call you back so soon, Raine," Andrea said quickly, "but Ebersole is waiting for an answer . . . like right now. They are anxious to get going on this. I know you haven't had much time to think about it, but we really need an answer. And please let it be yes."

I sighed and glanced over at Hayden who seemed to be looking at me more than the road.

"I can't, Andrea," I finally said. "I've made my decision and I'm set on it. My life is here." When I said the last, Hayden moved his arm from around me and rested his hand on his thigh. I looked at him as he stared straight ahead, his expression unreadable.

"I'm sorry, Andrea, but I have to go." I could tell she was annoyed with me, but at the moment I didn't care. One day I would try to help her understand my decision, but for now, I owed Hayden an explanation before he jumped to the wrong conclusion.

"So," he finally said after a minute, "you wanna to tell me what that was about?"

I looked at him and nodded. "Could we wait until we get there?"

"Fine," was his solitary reply.

Except for the country music station Hayden turned on to fill the silence, nothing else was said until we reached the lake.

A hurt of the heart is as indescribable as verbally painting a picture of a sunset for a person who has never seen color.

Thirteen

We were sitting on a blanket, each of us holding a cup of lemonade, when I began to tell Hayden about the call. I told him about the offer and what my decision had been. Through my whole explanation, he hadn't said a word. He just continued to stare out over the lake. When I finally finished, he surprised me by turning to look at me. My own eyes had never left his face the entire time.

"So, why didn't you tell me this morning?" Even as he asked, I saw something in his face that wasn't there before. I saw a storm brewing behind those beautiful gray eyes.

"I didn't say anything because I had already made up my mind. I don't want the job."

He heaved a deep sigh and pushed a hand back through his long tousled hair. "Well, at least now I know what was wrong when you came out earlier."

When he became silent again, I hurried on. "Hayden, listen to me. Really listen. My mind was made up as soon as she asked me. There was no question as to what I would say." I touched his arm. My life is here, with you." I took his large hand in mine. "You are the most important thing in the world to me."

"That's a lot of money, Raine. You sure you can turn it down just like that? I mean, you must have at least considered it."

I tucked a spiraled lock behind my ear, wishing I had brought something to tie my hair back. But then again, Hayden loved it when I wore my hair down.

"Truthfully, I was flattered. No, actually flattered is an understatement. I was seriously thrown for a loop to be made such an offer. But I was never tempted."

Hayden tossed a pebble out across the water. "Still, you didn't tell me." He looked at me. "I feel like you were purposely keeping it from me."

"I wasn't keeping anything from you," I said, not liking the way that sounded. I sighed painfully. "Hayden, please don't accuse me of something I'm not guilty of. I love you and I would never try to keep anything from you. It just wasn't important to me. If I had truly been considering it, believe me, you would've been the first to know."

He drew his long, lean legs up and wrapped his arms around his knees. After a couple of moments filled with agonizing silence, he said, "I don't wanna hold you back, Raine. I don't wanna be the reason you give up that kind of money."

My heart was suddenly hammering in my chest. I couldn't believe he was saying these things. Trying to keep my voice calm, I said, "You're not holding me back. Give me a little more credit, will you? If I had wanted the job, I would have taken it. But I didn't." When his expression didn't change, I started to get a little angry. "When I really want to do something, Hayden, no one will keep me from doing it."

"What's that supposed to mean?" he asked, anger entering his voice as well.

"It means that I love you and I don't want to leave, and no amount of money or position will make me leave. I don't need it, and I don't want it. I only want you." I paused. "You're what I need."

He said nothing, but I saw a flicker of softening in his eyes. Taking advantage of that moment, I moved closer and touched his face. "I love you, Hayden." He remained silent and my frustration worked its way to the surface once more. "Please don't push me away. I didn't do anything wrong and I don't deserve this."

He turned to me then, and I was startled by the hard look in his eyes. "No, you don't deserve this. You deserve better, a lot better than me." He stood. "Call them back and take the job, Raine. We can call everything off."

My heart instantly dropped. "What do you mean?" My voice cracked. "What are you saying?"

"I mean I'm not gonna stand in your way. You deserve a lot better than me and this kind of life. You can have better if you go back."

I felt tears threatening, but I refused to let them come. I couldn't understand how things had come to this. How could two phone calls change our lives? Our plans? I stood up and moved to stand in front of him.

For a second, the conversation I had with Caroline earlier came back to me, but I quickly pushed it away. In my mind it couldn't be that simple. There had to be more to it and I was beginning to feel too angry to think rationally.

"This isn't about money, Hayden and you know it. I don't need money. This is about you pushing me away. I don't know why, but you are. You said you loved me. You said you wanted to marry me more than anything. Have you changed your mind? Are you having second thoughts? Are you suddenly scared to make the commitment? I mean, it's like . . . like this is your way of getting out of marrying me, of getting rid of me."

He said nothing but continued to look out over the lake, the furrow in his handsome brow deepening. At another time, I would long to lift my fingers and smooth it away.

Taken aback by his continued silence, another thought suddenly came to me. A thought that was so painful, yet to me, seemed so likely, I suddenly felt cold. I again pushed the intruding conversation with Caroline aside, coming to my own conclusions. That 'getting some attitude' emotion I had managed to rein in through the years was ready to cut loose. I felt the straps breaking. My eyes narrowed slightly as I looked up at him. Then I snorted, which I could tell definitely took him off guard.

"So, I guess you've dabbled in a little brown sugar and decided you'd rather go back to white. The new flavor has lost its excitement. Is that it?"

He winced as if he'd been slapped. "That's not how it is with me, Raine. You know that."

"I thought I knew you. I thought I knew you better than anyone, but I guess I was wrong." I paused, trying to keep a strong hold on my emotions, but I was quickly losing the battle. Even still, I was determined to keep my pride in tact. I pressed my palm against my forehead and shook my head. "I can't believe this," I muttered under my breath. "You know, in some ways you're no different than Jerome."

His piercing gaze snapped to mine and I saw anger flashing in his eyes. "Woman, don't you dare compare me to him! I would never cheat on you or treat you the way he did!"

"No, you wouldn't cheat on me, but you sure know how to make me feel the same way he did! Oh, I'm fine to make out and get your kicks with, maybe even eventually sleep with, but not good enough to commit to."

"That's not true, Raine." His voice broke slightly. "I could never use you that way. I just think this is for the best."

"What's for the best exactly? Telling me you don't want me before you end up stuck with me? Is that what you mean?" I took a deep breath and pressed my lips together tightly. I suddenly felt tired, and I needed to be away from him. I silently emptied the cups and put them back in the basket. Then I picked up the blanket and folded it. "Take me back, please."

He closed his eyes and sighed. "I never meant to hurt you, Raine."

Yeah, whatever. "I'm done talking. Just take me back."

If pain could be buried in a hole
in the ground, the earth would
be dead.

Fourteen

The ride back to the ranch was completely silent. When we reached Caroline's, I said nothing as I got out. There was nothing left to say. But as I watched Hayden take off up the driveway toward his house, I felt him literally yank my heart away and take it with him. And I knew I would never get it back.

I was numb as I entered the house. Caroline met me in the hallway. She took one look at my face and knew something had happened. Saying nothing, she took my hand and guided me to the living room. It wasn't until we sat on the couch and she put her arms around me that I began to fall apart. Once the tears started, I couldn't seem to stop them.

Caroline held me and rocked me while I cried. I couldn't believe this was happening. Hayden had completely pushed me away. For some reason he didn't want me anymore, and now I just wanted to die. I had never experienced anything so excruciatingly painful in my life. I loved him so much and I didn't know how I would be able to live without him. Even though I had been married before, Hayden truly was, without a doubt, my first love, and he would be my only one. There was no one else in the world for me but him.

When I could finally stop crying enough to speak, the only thing I was able to get out was, "Hayden doesn't want me anymore. He told me to go back to Atlanta." Just saying it brought more tears.

"What happened?" Caroline asked, handing me a box of tissue from the end table.

It was still another full minute before I could speak again. Then I told her about the second phone call and how upset Hayden was because I hadn't told him. I told her everything that was said between us.

By the time I was done, I felt a little relief having gotten it all out, but the pain was still prominent and cut through me like a knife.

"Raine, I want you to listen to me," Caroline said, taking my hand. "It's like I told you this morning. That man is scared, pure and simple. He's scared of losing you."

I sniffed and wiped my eyes. "I know what you said, but how can I believe that? He just spent half an hour telling me to go back to Atlanta and take the job. I tried and tried to tell him that I didn't care about the job, but he wouldn't listen."

"That's because he's running scared. He's trying

to make you leave now because he thinks he'll eventually lose you anyway." She sighed. "I know Hayden, Raine. I've been around him long enough to know what makes him tick. And as sure as I'm sitting here I know he's feeling that you'll one day get tired of this life and want to go back. So if he makes you want to leave now, it will save him the heartache of dealing with it later. I know it doesn't make any sense to you, but it does to him, and right now he's so scared of losing you, he's not thinking rationally, even though he thinks he is. I thought he was all right after our talk last night, but apparently I was wrong."

I closed my eyes and shook my head in frustration. "Can't he see that I love him too much to ever leave him? Doesn't he have any faith in me at all?"

"Faith doesn't have anything to do with his decision, Raine. That man has always been alone. And while I know he has had an experience or two with other women, you're the first one to truly not just turn his head, but turn his heart, too. You own that man, Raine, heart and soul. This is the first time in his life he has ever been in love. It's the first time he has ever been committed to anyone."

"You mean *was* committed."

"I mean *is*, only he doesn't realize it yet. But he will."

"So am I supposed to just wait for him until he finally realizes it?"

"If that's what it takes."

"I don't know if I can, Caroline. How can I stay

here, be here where he is and not be with him? It would tear me apart to see him every day. It would be too uncertain." I chuckled bitterly. "I guess Jerome was right."

"Right about what?" Caroline huffed. "I can't imagine that man ever being right about anything."

"He called me earlier to give me his unsolicited, yet coveted opinion on my decision not to go back to the agency." I shook my head as tears again filled my eyes. "He said he would give us a year, or rather he would give *me* a year before I got tired and wanted out of this life. Ironically, it's Hayden throwing in the towel, not me."

"Oh, Jerome can go suck on a cow pie!" she spat angrily.

I smiled. As always, Caroline's words concerning Jerome were choice. I heaved a deep sigh, not knowing which way to turn or what to do. "How do I do this, Caroline?"

She was quiet a moment before she spoke again. She looked into my eyes intently. "I know everything seems uncertain, but how much do you love him, Raine? How much are you willing to risk? Is he worth taking the chance?"

Her last question stopped me cold and caused me to think. I had already given up the chance to have something that had at one time been my dream. I had given it up for Hayden. I hadn't wanted that dream anymore. I had a new dream that completely obliterated the other and vanished it into nothingness.

Could I give up on a life with him so easily? Give up on our hopes? Our dreams together? Could he?

I again sighed painfully. But how could I stay? It would be too painful to stay. "I don't know if I'm up to it, Caroline. I don't know if I'm strong enough."

Absence makes the heart grow stronger.

Fifteen

I didn't see Hayden again that day, nor did I see him the next. He didn't come to David and Caroline's for meals and I hadn't caught a glimpse of his presence anywhere. I couldn't help wondering if it was for his benefit or mine that he'd made himself scarce. Probably both. In a way it was good because I needed the space. On the other hand, I missed him with a painful intensity that made my heart ache beyond measure.

I didn't wander out on the ranch that day as I normally did. I stayed inside and tried to keep busy by helping Caroline with the usual housework. Then I faced the hard task of putting my wedding things away without ruining my dress with my endless tears, and calling Mama. I didn't tell her the wedding was off, just postponed. I hadn't yet made up my mind what I would do.

Again, Mama didn't throw out a bunch of questions at me. She knew me well enough to know I was thinking things through. However, she did give me one piece of advice, which I took as heaven sent. It's the only explanation I could come up with, because she had no clue what was going on with us, yet she knew exactly what to say.

Her advice? "If you really love him, then do what you can to work it out. You two have been, and still are, in the process of merging two different worlds. The odds are stacked against you as it is. They always were. Don't let fear keep you apart. Just do what you can to work it out." And that was it.

On Saturday, the day Hayden and I were supposed to be married, I worked myself ragged, doing any and everything I could possibly do to keep him off my mind. By noon, I was so tired, I skipped lunch and took a long nap.

It was while I was napping that Hayden made a quick stop to say he would be gone for a few days.

"He's going down to Houston for a few days," Caroline told me when I came down that afternoon. "He said he's going to take care of some business." She sounded angry. "Funny, he couldn't tell me what that *business* was. When I asked him he just shrugged his shoulders and turned to leave."

"What did you say" I asked, wishing I had been

down when he stopped by. Just to see him again would have been enough for me right now.

"What did I say? I told him he was being a stubborn jackass." When I gasped, she added, "Then I told him to hurry back and get this settled."

I smiled tearfully, grateful for Caroline's friendship. And if it wasn't for David coming in at that moment, I probably would have burst into tears all over again.

"Oh, there you are, sleeping beauty," he said, giving me a hug and kissing Caroline's cheek. "Tom said to ask you if you wanted to take Ol' Red out for a ride. He's getting lazy and needs some exercise."

"I'd love to," I said, feeling a little brighter. I loved riding Ol' Red. He was my favorite of all the horses, and I figured going for a ride and thinking about Hayden would be a lot better than sitting around the house thinking about him.

I grabbed a bottle of water from the fridge, excused myself, and headed down to the stable. By the time I got there, Tom had Ol' Red saddled outside and ready to go.

"How are you today, boy?" I said softly as I caressed the horse's silky mane.

"He's been missing you," Tom said, giving me a sympathetic smile.

"Well, I'm glad someone misses me," I mumbled as Tom helped me up in the saddle.

"Oh, I'm sure somebody else is missing you now, too." He grinned. "Only he's too stubborn and pig headed to see it right now. But don't you worry none. A body can only go without food and water for so long before it gives out."

I suddenly found myself grinning back at the older man. "Are you saying I'm food and water?"

"Shoot, sugar, you're that boy's all you can eat and drink buffet."

I laughed, genuinely laughed for the first time in days. "Thanks, Tom. I really needed that."

"Any time," he replied before going back into the stable.

From the corner of my eye I saw Chris enter. He approached me with his hands in his pockets. "Want some company?" he asked, rubbing the horse's nose.

"No, thanks. I'm just going to ride a bit and clear my head."

He smiled. "You sure you really want to be alone?" He playfully brushed off his shoulder. "I got a good one to lean on if you need to."

Yeah, right, buddy. "Thanks, but I'll be fine."

"Hey, Chris," Tom called as Chris started to move closer. "Ken needs your help with the shoeing."

Giving a smile of gratitude to Tom, I quickly took Ol' Red's reins and headed out.

Distraction is a mercy.

Sixteen

I relished the breeze blowing through my hair as I rode Ol' Red across the fields. The freedom I felt was like therapy, because as I rode, I was able to slowly dust the cobwebs of clutter and confusion from my heart and mind.

In the end I knew what I wanted, what I needed, and what I couldn't bear to live without. And as I approached the spot where Hayden had spent hours repairing the fence line, that knowledge came through with absolute clarity.

"Hayden." I breathed his name into the breeze, wishing the wind could somehow carry my voice across the distance to him.

I closed my eyes as memories of the love we shared the last morning I was with him penetrated my heart, causing a tangible ache in me that brought immediate tears to my eyes. I again saw the love in his gray eyes as he looked at me. I felt the strength of his arms as he held me, could taste the warmth of his kisses when he pressed his mouth to mine. Even now I could almost feel the warmth of his lips against mine, the memory was so strong.

"He loves me, God," I whispered emotionally to the heavens. "I know he does." Heaving a deep sigh, I gazed toward the fence once more, knowing with absolute certainty that the desperate love I felt for him would never fade. I would love him forever.

"And I will wait for him," I whispered fervently, my thoughts resolute. "There's still a chance, and I will wait." It was all I could do. In my heart, I knew there was no other choice.

I spent the next afternoon riding Ol' Red as well. I got back just in time to help Caroline prepare dinner. She was already sitting at the table peeling potatoes to go with the pot roast that was cooking in the oven. I washed my hands, took another peeler from the drawer, and sat down to help her. She looked over and smiled.

"How was your ride?"

"It was good. I think I've really needed these rides."

Caroline nodded. "A good swift ride works wonders when it comes to clearing your thoughts."

"You're right about that," I agreed with a smile.

We peeled potatoes for a while in silence, both of us seeming to be lost in our own thoughts. In the distance, I could hear calves bawling. Looking out the window, I saw one of the hands hauling in a load of alfalfa for the horses.

I sighed. Life was still going on, despite the changes going on in our lives. In my life. In Hayden's. Life was still going on without him. *I* was going on without him. I had no choice.

I'd always considered myself a pretty strong person and was usually up to any challenge. I had always faced life head on and tried to put blinders aside. But as I sat at Caroline's table peeling potatoes, I felt completely vulnerable. Despite a failed marriage in the past, I had come through it all relatively okay. I had struggled against the voices that whispered daily at that time, telling me that I wasn't worthy of having happiness with anyone. Whispers that I wasn't good enough.

And now here I sat, peeling potatoes and waiting for the return of a man who held my happiness in the palm of his hand. Yes, I was more vulnerable than I had ever been in my life. But I was also filled with perseverance, drive, and enough love in my heart to see this through. Come what may, I *would* see it through.

Caroline's voice softly interrupted my pondering.

"Hayden called today."

I looked up abruptly, my heart leaping at the sound of his name. "How is he?" I managed to ask, wishing I had been there.

"He's all right," was all she said.

I kept looking at her expectantly, every part of me yearning to ask if he said when he was coming home.

"He didn't really say much else," she added, evidently reading my thoughts in my expression.

I lowered my eyes and continued peeling, my heart beginning to ache all over again. You would think that missing him would now be a part of me, fitting me like a comfortable pair of worn shoes. But each new day, each little thing, freshened the pain.

I was struggling to blink back the tears when Caroline softly said, "He did ask me one thing though," and my head again shot up.

She smiled. "He asked if you were still here." When I put the peeler down and failed miserably to choke back the sob that escaped, she said, "I think he expected you to be gone by now." She reached across the table and squeezed my hand.

"He still loves you, Raine. In fact, I think he probably loves you more now than he did before he left, and I know he's probably hurting just like you are. You just hold on a little longer. It won't be too much longer now. He'll come around."

I smiled as tears streamed down my face and my heart was again infused with renewed hope. "I pretty much live off your faith, you know."

She chuckled and smiled. "I know, honey. I know."

Heartache is a detriment to the soul.

Seventeen

It was Caroline's faith that got me through the next couple of days. Whenever I began to feel down, I would just think of Hayden's phone call and Caroline's positive words, and I was instantly lifted. When I did that, I was able to make it from one hour to the next, one minute to the next.

But three days after Hayden's call, I was again restless and no memories or thoughts could console me. I now missed him so much, the pain threatened to completely overwhelm me.

That afternoon I decided I needed to go for a drive and get out for a while. I didn't really know where I would go, but I needed to go somewhere. Anywhere. I just needed a break, a break from missing Hayden, if that was possible.

Caroline had gone out earlier that morning and

wasn't back yet. Not wanting her to worry, I left a note on the kitchen table. It only said I was going out for a while.

While everything inside me wanted to revisit the places Hayden and I spent so much time, I decided to do other things. There really wasn't much to do that we hadn't done already, so I decided to see a movie. In fact, I ended up watching two, back to back. The first was a comedy, the second, a bittersweet love story, which I promptly kicked myself afterward for choosing.

After the second movie–I figured I had better stop at two–I decided to grab something to eat at a fast food place, purposely avoiding the vicinity of *Red Lobster*.

It was a completely relaxing day. I was in no hurry to get anywhere because there was no one for me to go back to. That fact only served to renew the lonely ache I carried inside.

Later that afternoon, I spent an hour wandering around a department store. I didn't buy anything. I found no joy in shopping alone anymore.

I spent the last part of the day sitting on a bench at a community park, watching laughing children playing on the swings and monkey bars. This activity was a huge mistake, because as soon as I sat down, my thoughts immediately drifted to the talks Hayden and I had about children. We had spent many moments daydreaming together about the children we wanted to have and what they would look like.

I closed my eyes and thought about the first time we discussed children. Well, it really wasn't a discussion. Hayden had pressed one of his large, gentle hands against my stomach and said, "I can't wait until my babies are growing inside you." Just thinking about the way he'd said it and the warmth in his eyes brought a warm longing even now.

"Oh, Hayden," I whispered. "I miss you so much. And I need you so badly it hurts." I looked up at the blue clear sky, wrapped my arms around my middle, and groaned painfully. *I'm going out of my mind, Hayden!*

I brushed away the sudden tears that came and took my keys from my pocket, my eyes catching the faint sunlit shimmer of Hayden's extra house key hanging from the ring with my car keys. He had given me the key the day he revealed his feelings for me in the stable.

I separated the key from the others and held it up. I sat for a moment staring at it and pondered all it represented. Suddenly feeling the need to feel as close to Hayden as I could, I quickly went to my vehicle and headed for the ranch.

By the time I reached the ranch, the sun had

gone down. I found Caroline and David relaxing in the living room. She was knitting and he was reading the paper.

"Sorry I was gone so long."

"That's all right," Caroline said, putting her knitting down. "You probably needed the time away."

"I did," I said with a sigh.

David flipped the top of his paper down. "So, how are you doing, darlin'? You all right?"

I pushed my hair back. "Truthfully, I don't know. I don't know when or if I'll ever be all right."

Caroline sighed. "You will." She paused. "Hayden called again."

I leaned my head against the door frame. "What did he say?" I asked in a monotone voice, expecting her answer to be the same as the last time.

"Well," she drawled, causing my heart to thump. "He asked me if you were still here . . . and I told him I didn't know where you were." When my eyes widened, she added, "Well, I *didn't* know where you were. Besides, he sounded pretty upset when I told him." She grinned. "I think you've got him scared, honey."

I couldn't help the joy I felt knowing Hayden was upset over my absence. "Did he say when . . . when he would be back?"

Caroline's smile faded slightly. "I'm sorry, honey, but he didn't."

The hope that I had just felt was dashed a little. "Well, I'm glad he's all right." I again pushed a hand back through my hair. "I think I'll go for a walk, maybe walk up to Hayden's." I smiled tearfully. "I kind of miss the porch swing."

"We understand," Caroline said. "We'll leave the door unlocked for you."

I nodded emotionally and left.

I stood on the back porch for a moment looking out over the ranch. With thoughts of Hayden ever present in my mind, I started my walk up to his place. I kept telling myself that going there would most likely only cause me more pain, but my heart wasn't listening. It didn't care. Besides, I didn't think the pain could get any worse than it already was.

Hearing the squeak of a door opening, I glanced back and saw Chris exiting the bunkhouse. I cursed inwardly when he looked in my direction and ran to catch up with me. I really wasn't in the mood to talk to him or anyone else, but especially *him*. Still, I managed to force a smile when he reached me.

"How are you doing?" he asked, reaching out and touching my arm.

"I'm all right," I lied. I smiled brightly. "I'm good."

When he moved closer, my smile faded slightly. Chris was nice, but a little too forward, and he was the last person I wanted to discuss my problems with. I turned to start walking when he abruptly took my arm in his hand, tightening his grip slightly. The action completely startled me.

"You're lying, Raine. I've got eyes. I see what's going on. Hayden deserted you and you're still determined to wait for him to come back."

I looked at him, my brow automatically creasing in anger and my defenses instantly rising. "So, what's it to you?"

"I'll tell you what it is to me," he said, moving even closer and causing me to back up a little. "I've been watching you. You didn't know it, but I have. You see, the way I figure it, you need a real man, and from what I can tell, Hayden definitely ain't man enough for the job. He can't handle a woman like you."

I snorted incredulously, my eyes roaming over his face, taking in his slicked back black hair and dark eyes. He was of average build and maybe six feet in height at the most. He was a couple of years younger than me, but at that moment, he acted even younger. "I don't know who you . . ." I paused and thought about what he had just said. "A woman like me? What is that supposed to mean?"

He smiled widely. "You know, a woman of color, or whatever you all call yourselves these days."

I shook my head slightly. *This is unreal.* "A woman of color, huh? Are you saying black women are different from white women?"

"I'm saying," he answered, his voice growing more seductive, "Hayden ain't man enough to give you what you really need."

"And what is that?" I asked with a smirk, sarcasm lacing my voice.

"Real loving. The kind you women like."

I'm not going to even touch that one. "Well, I hate to burst your bubble of raw masculinity," I finally said, way past bored with the conversation, "but Hayden is more of a man than you could ever hope to be."

"You think so, huh?" When I smiled, his expression changed. His hand shot out and grabbed my other arm, pinning them both behind me.

"Let go of me!" I yelled, more angry than scared. I struggled to free my arms but I couldn't get loose. His grip was solid.

"You know what I think?" he said, pressing me against him. "I think you need me to show you what a real cowboy can do for you."

Then before I could turn my head his repulsive mouth was on mine. I continued to struggle, but I couldn't break free of his grip. I finally bit down hard on his bottom lip, instantly drawing blood. The action caught him off guard and his grip loosened just enough for me to send a knee to his groin. He instantly doubled over. I hit him on the head once for good measure.

"Don't ever touch me again!" I yelled, quickly taking off toward Hayden's house. I looked back only once and sighed with relief when he staggered back down to the bunkhouse. I couldn't believe he'd acted that way. I wiped the blood from my mouth and shook my head.

Arrogant little jerk!

When I reached the front porch, I closed my eyes and took a deep breath, still stunned by what had just happened. No one had ever treated me that way before. I had known some bold men in Atlanta, but none were bold enough to attempt what Chris just did. I shuddered to think what Hayden would have done had he still been at the ranch. He would have beaten him senseless. At least Chris had had the sense to not push it further. Of course the good kneeing he received probably had something to do with that.

Pressing a palm against my forehead, I sighed and did my best to shake it off, then I faced the front door. Now that I had arrived, I was nervous about going in. I wasn't sure if my heart could handle it. Taking another deep breath, I pulled the key from my pocket and stuck it in the lock.

The worth of happiness isn't truly appreciated until it disappears, then reappears.

Eighteen

Standing in the living room of Hayden's home, I breathed in deeply the fresh scent of wood, pine, and leather. His scent, which normally mingled with the others, was absent. I missed his scent. I craved it.

I slowly walked down the hallway past a guest room and paused at the door of Hayden's bedroom before entering. Heaving an emotional sigh, I let my gaze travel around the room. This room was definitely Hayden. There were signs of him everywhere. From the faded brown western hat on the tall wooden bedpost, to the framed print of a cowboy on a bucking bronco, to the western decorative throw draped across the bottom of the beige down comforter set on the high king-size bed. He was everywhere.

I walked over to the dresser and picked up the bottle of *Stetson* cologne. He always wore it when we were together in the evenings. I smiled as I remembered him telling me that when he wasn't with me, there was no point in wearing it. It made me feel so special. I opened the bottle and lightly inhaled the scent, unprepared for the rush of emotion it brought. I quickly closed it and placed it back on the dresser. Then I remembered my main reason for coming in his room in the first place.

I walked over to the bed and picked up his pillow. Hugging it against me, I pressed my face into it and breathed in the scent that was his. It seeped into my senses and made me crave his gentle touch and loving caresses even more. I looked around the room a final time before taking the pillow and returning to the living room.

I knew that I should head back to David and Caroline's, but I couldn't bring myself to leave. Instead, I placed the pillow on the leather couch, took off my boots, and curled up, placing the pillow snugly beneath my head. I was so tired. Not just physically tired, but emotionally exhausted as well. I was tired of missing Hayden, tired of being alone, and tired of trying not to lose hope in the face of the uncertainty I felt each day.

"I'm so tired, Hayden," I whispered into the pillow. "I'm so tired."

Slowly waking from a deep sleep, I unconsciously leaned into the warmth I felt against my face, relishing the comfort it gave. Sighing, I slowly opened my eyes.

"Hayden," I breathed. Except for the moonlight shining through the curtains it was dark, but I would know his outline anywhere. He knelt before me, and I was immediately overwhelmed by his presence. Suddenly remembering where I was, I sat up and brushed the hair back from my face. "I'm sorry . . ." I cleared my throat, trying to get rid of the raspy tone in my voice. "I know I shouldn't be here. I'll go." When I tried to get up, he placed a gentle hand on my arm to stop me. At his touch, I heard the beat of my heart hammering in my ears.

"Don't leave." His voice quivered with emotion. "Please, baby, don't ever leave me."

I swallowed hard against the tears of joy in my throat, but I couldn't stop the sob that escaped. I couldn't believe he was there, that he wanted me to stay. It was too good to be true.

I pressed my hand to his cheek and caressed it as his tears wet my palm. Feeling his hands move to my waist, I took his face between my hands and our mouths instantly fused together. He pressed me tightly to him. His kisses were hot and fevered, and the sensation sent my mind and heart into emotional overload. We drank of each other, desperately trying to quench our thirst but unable to. The same words tumbled through my head over and over.

I love you. I love you. I love you. Please don't ever leave me again. Please don't. I need you, I need you . . .

He heaved a raspy sigh as his moist kisses traveled down my neck, just above the opening of my shirt and I suddenly felt as if I was on fire. He could have asked me for anything at the moment and I would have freely given it. I wouldn't have been strong enough to resist.

"Promise me you won't leave me," he whispered against my lips. "Promise me, baby. I won't lose you. I can't."

"You won't," I whispered back. "I promise. I won't ever leave you."

His arms immediately tightened around me and I felt my very soul being drawn into his. My entire being was trapped in the blissful, intoxicating world of his love, a world I never wished to escape.

After another moment of mutual feeding upon fevered kisses, he released my lips, pressed his face against my shoulder and cried. I leaned back against the couch and held him as he wrapped his arms around my waist and sobbed. My heart ached for him, yet I was filled with joy at the same time. I still couldn't believe he was really there, that I was really wrapped in his arms.

After a long while, he raised up and pressed his forehead to mine. I relished the feel of his warm breath on my face and dried the tears still falling down his.

"I've been so stupid, Raine. I've been so stupid about everything." He drew back a little. "Please let me explain."

"You don't have . . ."

He pressed a finger to my lips, then replaced it with his mouth and I couldn't resist tangling my fingers in his hair and pulling him closer. "Yes I do," he finally said, breathless. "And baby, please don't kiss me again until I say this or I won't be able to think." I smiled and nodded, thrilled that I still had the same effect on him.

"The day you said you would be mine, I felt like the most blessed man in the world, and when you agreed to marry me, my world was perfect. But then I started worrying that my love wouldn't be enough to keep you here, that it wouldn't be enough to make you happy and you would get tired of life here."

His voice was full of pain as he poured his soul out to me and I wanted so badly to take it all away. I realized now that I hadn't been suffering alone while we were apart.

He sighed deeply. "You know, I actually managed to convince myself that I was just being foolish until you got that call from the agency. I kind of lost it after that. I was so afraid of losing you, I couldn't think rationally. I couldn't think, period. I knew I was hurting you, but I couldn't see past my own fear." He paused and I could hear the tears filling his voice again.

"Please forgive me, Raine. Forgive me for being so awful to you, for not trusting you and your love for me." He caressed my face. "Please forgive me for leaving, for being such a coward, for everything."

I smiled and pressed my hand into his hair. Oh, how I had missed doing that! "I do forgive you, Hayden," I whispered before touching my lips lightly to his. "I'm just so glad you came back, and that you still love me."

"Baby, I'll always love you. I'll love you forever." He then fully captured my mouth with his again and favored me with another warm kiss.

I was again drowning in a delirium of overwhelming passion as he scattered hot kisses all over my face and hungrily took my mouth again. It was as if we were both trying to make up for lost time. I couldn't hold him close enough, couldn't kiss him enough. I had been deprived of his kiss, his touch, and his warmth for too long, and I couldn't seem to satisfy my hunger for him. Everything inside me ached to be completely his. I needed him with a painful intensity that made my whole being ache.

I finally pressed my face to his shoulder. "I've missed you so much," I said, shedding tears of happiness and gratitude.

"I've missed you, too," he murmured into my hair, holding me close. "You're all I could think about. When Caroline said she didn't know where you went, I thought you had left and I almost lost it."

Pulling back slightly, I caressed his beard. "I would have waited forever for you, Hayden." I swallowed against the emotion in my throat. "Don't you know you mean everything to me?"

He sighed and again tightened his embrace. Burying my face in the hollow of his neck, I pressed several kisses there and he moaned softly. I could feel his pulse racing. He was warm, he smelled so good, and his arms were so safe.

After a moment, he released me and moved to the end of the couch to turn on the lamp. Then he knelt in front of me again, letting his eyes travel the length of me, his gaze as soft and warm as a caress.

"What's this?" he asked, fingering the smear of blood on my shirt. I hadn't even noticed it until that moment.

"It's nothing," I said, looking away.

"Raine." The tone of his voice instantly commanded my attention. "Where did this come from?"

I sighed, knowing there was no way of skirting around the answer. I knew I couldn't lie to him. "Well, Chris sort of made me an offer that I refused, despite his attempt to convince me otherwise."

Hayden instantly took my shoulders in his hands and his eyes narrowed. "What did he do to you?"

I put a calming hand on his chest, startled by the mad thumping of his heart. "He just said some things and . . ."

"And what?"

I heard the rising anger in his voice and I felt his muscles go tense. I again hesitated.

"What did he do?" he asked again in a voice that demanded the truth.

"He pinned my arms behind me and . . . he kissed me." When Hayden stood up and swore, I reached for his hands and squeezed them tightly and

161

hurried on. "I bit his lip and he loosened his grip enough for me to knee him good and get away."

"That lousy little . . . He roughly ran a hand back through his hair and swore again. "Son of a . . . I'll kill him! I swear I will!"

"Hayden, no!" I said, standing and taking his face in my hands. He squeezed his eyes shut and I felt his whole body trembling with rage. "Hayden, look at me," I continued softly. "I'm all right. Everything is okay."

I continued to caress his face. "I'm all right," I repeated over and over again, trying to calm him down. After another moment he took a deep breath and finally opened his eyes, looking down at the blood on my shirt again. "You must've bitten him pretty hard." A slight smile touched his lips.

"I did." I knew he was still upset, but at least he was calmer.

Taking his hands in mine, I sat back down and he knelt in front of me again and softly caressed my face, brushing a thumb across my lips. "I hate the thought of anybody else touching you," he growled. "I don't want anybody else touching you."

"No one else will," I whispered as I leaned forward and kissed his lips.

He pulled me tightly against him and deepened the kiss so much, it was almost as if he was trying to erase both Chris' kiss and his touch from my memory. He didn't realize he had already done that without even trying. All it took was him just being there when I had awakened.

He drew back and pressed his hand into my hair. "I miss doing this," he whispered. "When I touch you, it feels like home." His eyes roamed over my face. "You're so beautiful."

I looked into his eyes and smiled. "So are you."

"You know, I promised God that if He would just let you still be here when I got back, I would never hurt you again, and I intend to keep that promise." Tears again filled my eyes as he gazed at me intently. "Let's get married tomorrow, Raine. The blood tests and everything have been done. We could get Reverend Collier out here and just do it." When I smiled, he again ran a thumb over my trembling lips. "I don't want to wait any longer to make you mine, Raine. Completely mine."

"I don't want to wait either," I finally managed to say. "But," I added with a grin, "since it's two o'clock in the morning, I think we should give Caroline at least one more day to be prepared, don't you?"

I laughed as he groaned and pressed his face to my neck. "I guess we should. She's probably already gonna have my hide as it is for leaving in the first place. I guess I owe her that much." When I nodded in agreement, he sobered and a hint of sadness again entered his eyes. "Raine, I . . ."

I pressed my fingers over his lips. "You're here now. Nothing else matters."

He took my face in his hands. "I promise I'll make you happy, baby."

"I know," I said before his kiss again melted through my insides like warm molasses.

Hayden was home. He was mine. And the world was right again.

Later on that morning, I stood by and watched Hayden physically pick Chris up and toss him out of the bunkhouse along with his personal belongings. He told him to get off the property and never come back. The rest of the hands stood close by as backup for Hayden. Not that he needed it. They considered themselves family, and I was a part of that family. The next day, it would be official.

J. Adams

Nothing improves the silence
like the sound of a lover's
pledge!

Nineteen

I wore a teary smile as I stood with my hand in Hayden's beneath a white linen gazebo that had been set up on the side of David and Caroline's home. Vases of white roses surrounded us, their scent filling the air and adding an extra sweetness to the occasion.

I wore a white, silky wedding dress that I'd bought off the rack and Hayden wore a new dark blue suit. We were surrounded by the people closest to us as we exchanged vows and pledged our love to each other.

The moment Hayden and I exchanged the beautifully etched gold bands and were pronounced husband and wife, I knew true happiness for the first time in my life. In that moment, I became his, he became mine, and our lives were instantly merged.

Tears of joy slipped down my cheeks as he took

me in his arms and kissed me whispering, "I love you, baby," as our lips parted. He pressed a hand to my face, brushing a tear away. "And I'm all yours, Mrs. McKade."

I nodded, unable to speak at the moment, but I was sure he knew what was in my heart.

David and Caroline showered us with hugs and congratulations. Tom and the rest of the men shook Hayden's hand and slapped him on the back heartily. They each hugged me and pressed a kiss to my cheek. Hayden told them to enjoy it because they would never get to kiss me again and they all laughed.

After having some cake and punch, Hayden quickly swept me up in his arms, said thanks to Reverend Collier and everyone else, and carried me out to the truck. Before we drove off, he called out the window, "We'll see ya'll in two days. If anybody knocks on our door before then, you're dead."

I laughed as the guys hooted and yelled wise cracks, some of which, would have caused me to blush had my skin tone been lighter. As we drove off, I waved to Caroline, returning her teary smile with one of my own. Then I turned to my new husband and smiled, warmed by the complete love I saw in his eyes.

When we reached the house, Hayden carried me in and locked the door. He took my hand and we walked back to the bedroom. Standing next to the bed,

Hayden stood for a moment, silently gazing down at me and I could almost read his thoughts as easily as I could read the love and desire in his eyes.

"I can't believe I really have you," he finally said. "I can't believe you're mine."

I reached up to touch his beard, but my fingers settled on his lips instead. "I can't either."

"I have ached to have you for so long, to be with you like this."

"I have wanted you, too. More than you know."

He continued to gaze down at me quietly for a another minute before turning and pulling back the covers.

I looked up at him in nervous anticipation and I sensed that he was a little nervous too. I smiled and turned my back to him, lifting my hair for him to undo the buttons on my dress. I felt tingly with each button he undid.

"Raine," he breathed into my hair, taking my shoulders in his gentle hands and turning me to face him. "It's been a long time for me." His voice was low and raspy.

I took one of his hands in mine and kissed it. "That is the best wedding present you could ever give me." I pressed my hand against his chest and felt the pounding of his heart. "You are the love of my life, Hayden McKade. And you will be the last man I ever give myself fully to. I am completely yours."

He smiled at me tearfully. When he spoke again, I could hear the deep emotion in his voice. "Woman, you completely own me, heart, mind, body, and soul. And you always will."

There were no more words between us. Staring into each other's eyes, we undressed, slipped beneath the cool covers, and we loved.

Never in my life could I have ever guessed that love, passion, and ecstasy could produce an experience that was so fulfilling, so unearthly that it literally gave me the sense of being lifted to a higher plane. I never dreamed a body could experience them all at once. But I did, with his every touch, his every kiss, and his every softly whispered word. When we finally became one, I reached an even higher plane, a plane that I never knew existed.

Then we held each other, never wanting to let go, and I was amazed.

A love that has been tested is an
inspiring thing to behold.

Twenty

I turned to my side, propped up an elbow and rested my head against my hand as I lay watching Hayden watching me. He lay on his back. He was so relaxed, and his eyes held the intoxicating look of love. I pressed my hand to his face and smiled. He smiled back and continued to quietly gaze at me.

"You probably won't believe this, but you've made me a mother today, Hayden."

He grinned. "And just how do you know that, darlin'?"

"I just know."

He turned on his side and propped himself up on his elbow. "You really want a baby, don't you?"

I nodded. "I've dreamed of nothing else since the day you told me how you felt about me in the stable. Well, actually I started thinking about it the moment you walked into the stable eating that strawberry."

"Really?" he said, grinning wider. "You were dreaming about having my babies even then?"

I nodded, smiling at his playful grin. "I picture us with a half dozen kids or so running around this place."

"Half dozen, huh. Well, I guess it's a good thing I built big."

"It is," I agreed, thinking about how much work he had put into building the five bedroom home. I sighed softly and placed my hand on his arm, feeling the firm muscles beneath his tanned skin. "Our boys will be strong and handsome like their daddy."

He pulled me into his arms. "And our girls . . ." He paused and kissed my lips lightly. "Our girls will be beautiful like their mama."

I wrapped my arms around his waist and kissed him then, and all conversation ceased as the passion between us flared once more.

That evening we finally got up and ate a light meal. Then, wrapped together in a blanket, we sat out on the porch swing and talked. It was another cool evening, but we had each other to keep warm.

Hayden held me close and I rested my head against his shoulder.

"You know your mama's gonna have my hide for not giving her time to get here for the wedding."

"Naw," I drawled. Hayden's speech was slowly rubbing off on me. "I think she will just be happy we worked things out."

"She's not the only one."

I nodded and looked up at him. "I love you, Mr. McKade."

"And I love you, Mrs. McKade."

I brushed my thumb against his lips as he lowered his head and kissed me. Each time he kissed me, touched me, or even looked at me, I could feel his love wash over me, and the warmth of it consumed my very soul. As his kiss deepened, my whole being yearned to melt into him.

"Raine," he whispered as his mouth continued to passionately coax mine. "I'll make you happy. I promise I will."

I eased back a little and looked into his eyes. "You've already made me happier than you could ever know."

He pressed his mouth to mine again. "You're everything to me, Raine," he continued to whisper. "You're everything."

I sighed and burrowed further into his embrace. His arms tightened around me as he pressed his face into my hair. We held each other in silence. No more words were needed. We just let our hearts do the talking. We ended that night and the next, sitting on the porch swing, reveling in our love, and anticipating our future.

Life is grander when you can
share it with your soul mate.

Twenty-one

Over the next few days, I settled into my new home by adding some much needed decor. I started the transformation by adding wildflower arrangements here and there. I hung some southwestern prints on the walls and added thick woven area rugs to each room. I placed a large scented jar candle on a warmer in the kitchen. It made the whole house smell like pumpkin and spiced apples. I also bought a stereo for the living room, and Hayden quickly made it a house rule that we share at least one dance each night. I loved that rule.

In our bedroom, I placed a large vase of silk sunflowers on the dresser, and another on a round, dark wood table in the corner. Other than my toiletries in the bathroom along with new matching towels, my clothes in the walk-in closet with Hayden's, and a few framed photos of Hayden and me here and there, nothing else had been changed. The room was still Hayden, with a feminine touch.

Hayden told me he loved what I did with the house. He said it felt more like home to him now, not just because of the things I had added, but because I was there. He always melted my heart when he said things like that.

The next week we flew to California for a few days and went to Disneyland. Neither of us had ever been there before and were excited about going. It was also the first time I had ever seen Hayden in anything except Wranglers and boots. Dressed in knee-length denim shorts, exposing his muscular calves, a tan, form fitting t-shirt, and a pair of Nike sneakers, he was completely and utterly adorable. I had also bought myself some denim shorts and cap-sleeved t-shirts for the trip, as well as a pair of Mary Jane Sketchers so I would be comfortable waking around the park in the hot sun.

We spent two days at the park, going from ride to ride. Fortunately, I took a tube of motion sickness pills with me, so I was able to handle the rides pretty well and I had a lot of fun. At the end of both days, we left the park with bags of souvenirs to take back home.

We spent our last day in California at the hotel. Earlier in the day we went for a swim in the pool, or rather Hayden went for a swim. I just walked around in the shallow end. Though the water felt good, I told myself that one day I would indeed learn how to swim.

Truthfully, Hayden spent more time admiring me in my bathing suit than he did swimming. And he always managed to stay close by to fend off any male guests that came my way. All he had to do really was get out of the pool and walk his massive body toward me, and that usually got rid of anyone who stopped to chat. I had to smile whenever he did that, and it made me love him all the more.

We lay by the pool and let the sun dry us for a while, then we went back up to our suite and ordered room service.

I sat on the sofa next to Hayden, wrapped securely in his arms.

"Thank you, for bringing me here, Hayden. I've had so much fun."

"You're welcome, darlin'," he said, pressing a kiss to my brow. "We'll have to come again sometime."

"I'd like that." I looked up at him and smiled mischievously. "Just to see you in shorts again would make the whole trip worth it."

"Is that right?" he said, grinning and tightening his embrace.

"Definitely." I reached up and pressed a hand to his face, softly brushing my thumb across his lips.

"Well, I wouldn't mind seeing you in that bathing suit again either."

"Tell you what," I whispered as I pulled his head down and touched my lips to his. "How about I put it on each day and greet you at the door when you come home?"

He eased back and smiled widely. "Darlin', if you did that, them meals you work so hard to cook every day would go to waste, because we'd be too busy to eat."

I chuckled. "This is true." I looked into his eyes and sobered. "I love you. Thank you for marrying me, and for loving me so much."

He smiled lovingly and swallowed hard. When he finally spoke, there was emotion in his voice. "I love you, too, baby. And thank you for not giving up on me. On us." He gently cupped my face and lowered his mouth to mine, kissing me slowly, tenderly. I sighed as the kiss deepened and I was quickly lost in the passion between us. With each whispered word from his lips against mine, I was pulled further away from the world around us and deeper into his, into the one his love created for me. And it was in that world that I knew I would always stay.

Heaven can be mirrored in a
simple phrase.

Twenty-two

I stood at the kitchen sink, scrubbing a frying pan I had just used to cook pork chops for dinner. I expected Hayden to come through the door at any minute, and because of feeling sick earlier in the day, I had fallen behind. But I did manage to have dinner ready on time.

I smiled as I thought about my handsome husband. He made the past two months the happiest of my life. I never dreamed marriage could bring such contentment, but I guess being married to someone I loved with all my heart and soul helped.

Drying the frying pan, I stood for a moment and thought about my life. Compared to the past, my life now was a simple one. There were no modeling jobs to run off to, no hair or nail appointments, and no business lunches with perspective clients.

Instead, I got up each morning and made breakfast for Hayden. I took care of his house, made his lunch, did his laundry, cooked his dinner, and anything else I could do to make him happy and be the best wife I could be to him. The reward for my efforts could not be put into words, because every time he came through that door and took me in his arms and said, "I've missed you, baby," my world was perfect.

I again smiled as I pressed a hand against my flat stomach. I had news for Hayden that would not only change our life, it would complete it. I longed to share the news with Mama as well, but I needed to tell my husband first. And oh, how excited Mama would be when she found out!

I gazed out the window across the rolling acres of green as memories of Mama's visit three weeks before filled my mind. It had been so good to see her. I smiled as I remembered her hugging Hayden first thing and telling him how grateful she was to him for marrying me and making me so happy. He told her it was the other way around. Mama had grinned widely when Hayden told her that he could see where I got my beauty. She told him he was quite the charmer and I agreed completely.

Hayden decided that he couldn't call Mama Hannah, her first name, because it would be too impolite, so he started calling her Mama, which suited her fine.

I chuckled as I remembered Mama telling Hayden how good looking he was. He had grinned widely, then leaned down and kissed her cheek, whispering loud enough for me to hear, "I think that's why your daughter fell for me. Of course, I did have my shirt off the first time she met me, which probably helped."

I immediately gasped, embarrassed. He only grinned and pulled me close.

Mama laughed and said, "Well, she definitely must have liked what she saw. And anybody that can bring an unseen blush to Raine's cheeks the way you just did must be doing something right."

"I do my best," Hayden had replied with a chuckle.

We gave Mama a tour of the fair town of Roswell and showed her some sights. And she hooted with laughter even more than I did when we took her to the UFO Museum.

Caroline and David loved seeing Mama again and we all had dinner a couple of times at their house. And while the men worked during the day, Caroline and I took Mama around the ranch and showed her what we did there. All in all, it had been a wonderful and memorable visit. She promised me before she left that she would come again.

The only dark spot to mar an otherwise perfect two months was the delivery of a wedding gift from Jerome, a so-called peace offering. The gift itself would have been very nice if not for the meaning behind it. The gift, a gold-plated place setting for four, was accompanied by a card in which Jerome congratulated us and casually remarked that he wouldn't want me to miss out on the good things in life, so he sent the place setting to remind me of the life I gave up. He also bragged in the card that he was now dating the model who was the new face of Ebersole.

And what was Hayden's response to receiving the gift? He burned the card and gave the place setting away. So, that took care of that.

Pulling my thoughts to the present, I watched a hummingbird as it fluttered near and drank the sweet nectar in the bird feeder Hayden had hung from a hook by the window. I don't know why, but in that moment I suddenly began to wonder if my life was too perfect. Things were so blissful that I suddenly felt sure there was a trial right around the corner. Not that we hadn't had our share of trials before, nor was I looking for trouble. It was just a feeling. I found myself praying it wouldn't be anything major.

This is silly, I mused. *You have a wonderful life, girl, so don't go looking for trouble. What's with this sudden bout of paranoia anyway?* I shook my head and smiled.

I started taking some dishes down from the cupboard when I heard the front door open and I immediately felt butterflies in my stomach. In the next instant, Hayden's warm arms came around me and he pressed a soft kiss against the side of my neck. I closed my eyes and snuggled deeper in his embrace.

"I've, missed you, baby," he said, pressing his lips to my ear and I sighed.

"I've missed you too." I turned to face him and

he leaned down, giving me a proper greeting.

"Mmmm," I murmured. "I've been waiting all day for that."

"And I've been waiting all day to do it."

"Why don't you go on and shower and I'll get dinner on the table."

"All right. Be back in a few." He kissed me again and headed to the bedroom.

While Hayden showered, I placed the food on the table and set it for two. I paused in my actions and thought with joy how wonderful it would one day be to be able to set three, four, even five more places at the table.

I took a pitcher of lemonade from the refrigerator and placed it on the table as well. Then I sat down and waited for Hayden. He came in a few minutes later, freshly showered, wearing clean jeans, and of course, shirtless and barefoot. I couldn't help thinking that he had to be the most irresistible man in the world.

"How was your day?" he asked as he sat down and pulled me close for another kiss.

"It's been good. Of course, it's always better when you come home."

He grinned. "It's the best time of the day for me, too."

I passed the plate of pork chops and he speared one and put it on his plate.

"I did get the flowers planted. The pots are on the deck."

"That's good, darlin'. I'll have to go out and take a look."

"It really did give me a feeling of accomplishment, especially since I have never planted anything before. I was always too busy to take care of plants. For me, silk flowers have always been the way to go. No way I can kill them."

He chuckled. "Well, I have faith that you'll keep these alive."

"I hope so. Caroline has a green thumb when it comes to gardening. Maybe it will rub off on me a little."

"You do well at everything you set your mind to."

"This is true," I said with a coy smile. "I got you, didn't I?"

"That you did, darlin'," he answered, his eyes full of love.

"And," I said, my voice softening and my insides bursting with happiness, "I have your baby growing inside me."

The fork in Hayden's hand stopped in the air midway to his mouth. He put it back on his plate as his eyes widened in wonder. "You're pregnant?" He grinned. "Really?"

I nodded, smiling. "Really."

He pulled me from my chair and onto his lap, and wrapping me in his arms, he pressed his face against my neck. "Raine," he breathed. "Oh, Raine. You've made me a happy man." He touched my face and moved his hand to my stomach, holding it there. "My baby," he whispered.

I pressed a hand to his face and kissed him warmly. "I love you."

"I love you." He kissed me another moment before standing and lifting me in his arms. "Dinner can wait."

I smiled, warmed by the desire burning in his gray eyes.

Old annoyances never disappear but tend to strike when you least expect.

Twenty-three

For the next couple of months, the morning sickness was almost unbearable at times. I spent more time lying in bed than I did doing anything else. I took Caroline's suggestion and tried to eat more small meals during the day, but it didn't really help because I could never keep anything down. I was miserable almost every waking moment.

Caroline helped out a lot by bringing in dinner so Hayden wouldn't go hungry, even though he told us both he was perfectly capable of fixing his own meals. He did, however, make his own breakfast in the mornings, and mine as well. If he knew he was going to be too busy to come home for lunch, he would make a couple of sandwiches to take with him. Each morning before he left, he brought a breakfast tray to me in bed. Then he would grab his own plate and come to the bedroom and eat with me. He felt terrible about having to leave, but I always assured him I would be all right.

After Hayden left in the mornings, I usually managed to take a shower and straighten the house a little. If I lay down in between, I could even get a couple of loads of laundry done. But by noon, I was always too sick again to do much else.

When Hayden came home in the evenings, he usually took a quick shower and we would have the dinner Caroline brought in. Afterward, he would climb into bed and hold me, and we'd talk until I fell asleep, which usually didn't take long. He made me feel so safe, and so loved. And I loved him and our unborn child more than I could say.

After another month, I started feeling better and was able to take care of my home and my husband again, and I really began to enjoy being pregnant.

Right after I had found out I was pregnant, I had gone into town that following day and purchased some maternity clothes, anticipating the day when I could finally start wearing them. And now that the day was here, I was glad that I bought them early. My clothes were now too tight to even button. I found that pretty amusing when I thought about all the times I had wished I could gain a few pounds.

To celebrate my freedom from being confined to the house, Hayden offered to take me shopping for baby clothes and things for the nursery. Since the baby's furniture had been ordered and delivered a couple of weeks before, I was excited about decorating it.

I put on a pair of slim fitting denim capris and a pink v-neck maternity shirt made with a stretchy material that accentuated my growing abdomen. Both pieces of clothing, as well as the rest of the maternity clothes, I had had to buy in the smallest size, so they fit pretty well. And I loved the way the pregnancy was already adding a little more curve to my figure. Hayden told me I looked beautiful, and I actually felt beautiful.

Later, I sat at the kitchen table with a cup of herbal tea and waited for Hayden. He was out on another part of the property checking the fence, but I expected him back soon. He was excited about taking me shopping and getting me out for a while. I really missed going out with him, too.

By the time I finished my tea, I had made up my mind to drive out to where Hayden was, but the telephone rang, stalling my plan.

"Raine, it's me."

"Hi," I said, immediately hearing the strain in Caroline's voice. "What's going on?"

"You're not going to believe this, but your ex is sitting downstairs in my living room."

"What?" I said in disbelief. "Jerome?"

"I know. I couldn't believe it either when I opened the front door and found him standing there like he was posing for the cover of GQ or something. He came struttin' in here as vain as a peacock."

"I don't believe this! What does he want?"

"Why, to see you, of course. He said he's on his way to Los Angeles for some business and just stopped by to say hello." Caroline's voice was dripping with sarcasm.

"Humph, just stopped by, huh?" I snorted. "Just stopped by my eye! Jerome has a motive for everything he does. And I don't know what makes him think I would want to see him anyway."

"Well," Caroline replied, "if truth be told, I think he just wants to check out his replacement, maybe stir up some trouble."

I closed my eyes and rubbed my temples. The last thing I needed or wanted was to see Jerome, and it really bothered me that he couldn't seem to stay out of my life.

This has got to stop. "I'm on my way down."

Against The Odds

Just when you think you have someone figured out, you realize that you actually do.

Twenty-four

Caroline met me at the back door. "I sent someone out for Hayden."

"Good," I said, then wondered if it really was good. As protective as Hayden was of me, meeting Jerome would definitely put him in a bone-breaking mood.

"You all right?" Caroline asked.

I nodded. Taking a deep breath, I headed to the living room. Caroline walked close behind me.

Jerome was standing by a window looking out over the land. When I entered, he turned and flashed that familiar sly smile. Instant nausea rolled through my insides as his eyes roamed over me, his gaze lingering for a moment on my stomach.

"I hope you don't mind me stopping by." He grinned, looking at me quietly for a moment. Taking in his devilish expression, I knew he was up to no good. "I was going to ask how you were doing," he finally said, "but . . . I can see you've been pretty busy." When I rolled my eyes he added, "Still, you look good."

"Thanks," I replied, not bothering to disguise the sarcasm.

He walked over to me. "So, how has life been treating you?"

"Just fine." I heaved an impatient sigh, bored with the small talk already.

"You plan on making it back to Atlanta any time soon?"

I looked over at Caroline's permanent frown and knew exactly how she felt. I massaged my temples, trying to relieve the ache in my head.

"Why are you here, Jerome? And don't tell me it's just to say hello. I know you better than that. Most men don't go out their way to see their ex-wives. In fact, most men don't even *want* to see their ex-wives."

He smiled. "Truthfully, I just wanted to see for myself what kind of life you gave up such a successful career for." He shook his head. "And I have to say, I do miss having you on my arm. We always looked good together."

This is unreal! "You are a piece of work, you know that? You're as full of yourself as you always were."

He chuckled, irritating me even more. "I just don't see how you could think you'd be happier here than in Atlanta, living the kind of life you're used to."

His eyes again roamed over me. "Where's the woman whose gorgeous body graced the fashion runways of Atlanta and made men weak in the knees? I mean, I still see that woman in front of me, though slightly altered in the body area, but what happened to her?"

Oh, you little jerk! I took a deep breath. "She found something better, Jerome. She moved on, which it what you need to do."

"Oh, I have," he said with arrogance.

"Have you? Have you really?" I stretched my arms out dramatically. "Well, if that's the case, then why are you here?"

He moved closer, a seductive smile playing on his lips, and I had to seriously wonder if he had lost his mind. "I told you. I had to see this for myself. *And* meet your old man, of course."

He placed a hand on my arm, his thumb caressing, and I suddenly felt dirty. "Jerome, if you value your life, you will take your hand off me."

He laughed. "Being a little melodramatic, aren't we? You never complained about my touch before."

"I am serious. Don't touch me." I tried to pull my arm away, but he held firm. I looked at my sister-in-law. "Caroline would you . . ."

There was no need to finish, because in the next moment we heard the kitchen screen door open and slam shut followed by heavy booted footsteps. Not bothering to turn around, I watched Jerome stumble backwards a little and his eyes widen as Hayden entered, his massive form filling the room. I wanted to laugh, but I just smiled and turned to my husband as he gently pulled me against him. Carefully masked anger creased his handsome brow slightly, and I felt the hard muscles of his chest flexing beneath the faded red t-shirt. His hat shaded his eyes, but I saw the hard glint in them.

"Hayden," I said, tightening my arm around his waist, "this is Jerome." I looked over at Jerome and couldn't help smiling at the startled expression he still wore. "Jerome, this is my husband, Hayden."

"Hello," Hayden said, unmoving, his arm tightening around my waist possessively.

"Good to meet you." Jerome's voice held a hint of wariness.

When both men continued to stand there staring at one another, I nervously cleared my throat and glanced at Caroline who shrugged her shoulders and shook her head, a slight smile playing across her lips. I looked up at Hayden and took his free hand in mine, urging him to look at me. When he did, the look in his eyes softened.

"Hayden, Jerome is on his way to California. He just stopped by to say hello." I glanced over at Jerome. "And now he is leaving."

Jerome smiled slightly and pushed his hands into the pockets of his designer slacks. "Yeah, I was just leaving." He looked at me and flashed another grin. "It's good to see you, Raine." He cut his eyes to Hayden, then back at me. "You really *have* changed, in more ways than one. No one at Zuri would recognize you."

I shook my head. "And I can see that when it comes to you, some things never change."

He smirked, and without another word, turned to leave.

Hayden released me and moved forward. Fearing what he might do, I nervously tried to hold on to his hand, but he gave mine a gentle squeeze and pulled away.

"Uh, Jerome?" When Jerome turned to us, Hayden loomed over him and said in that deep drawl of his, "This has been fun, but don't ever come here again. Raine is *my* wife now, and I always protect what's mine. Don't contact her in any way. No phone calls, no cards or letters. Nothing. You got that?" The tone of his voice was almost chilling.

Jerome's voice sounded smaller than I had ever heard it when he replied, "I got it." He quickly opened the door and left.

Hayden went to the window and watched Jerome get into his car, wanting to make sure he really was leaving. He didn't move from that spot until Jerome drove away. Shaking his head, he swore under his breath. "Idiot is what he is."

Caroline's chuckle startled me. "Well, I guess that boy encountered more than he bargained for."

I smiled. "I think he did."

Hayden walked back over to me and pulled me close. "Are you all right?" he asked, pressing his face into my hair.

I closed my eyes and nodded, feeling safe in his arms. "Maybe he will finally move on with his own life now and stay out of mine." I released a low chuckle. "He was moving on with other women when we were still together. I don't know what his problem is now." Jerome's actions never failed to puzzle, and annoy me.

Caroline sat on the sofa. "Well, I don't think you will have to worry about him anymore." She smiled widely at Hayden.

"I don't think she will either," Hayden agreed. He sighed, holding me tighter. "You know, it's hard for me to picture you married to him."

I drew back a little and smiled up at him. "It is for me, too, now. However, I *am* picturing you hanging him up in the barn by his Italian loafers."

Hayden chuckled and kissed me. "If he ever comes back, that will be some entertainment you can look forward to, all right?"

I nodded, grateful to be married to such an amazing man.

"All right, baby," he said, kissing my brow, "that's enough drama for this morning. Now let's go shopping."

I thoroughly enjoyed perusing the baby section of *Sears*. The opportunity to pick out things for our baby helped to take my mind off Jerome's surprise visit. It still bothered me that he came and I really hoped he got Hayden's message loud and clear about not contacting me again.

There were a lot of things we needed to get, so we each pushed a shopping cart.

Hayden helped me pick out some cute sleepers and blankets in neutral colors. We wouldn't know the sex of the baby for another week. After that I would go shopping again for the appropriate things. We filled the cart with diapers, t-shirts, and bedding that Hayden picked out, deciding on a horse theme. He said our baby would be a cowboy or cowgirl from the start.

"What do you think of this, darlin'?" he asked, holding up a small lamp with a porcelain horse as the base.

"I think it's perfect," I answered, smiling at the excitement in his eyes. He was like a kid at Christmas. And nothing was too good for our baby.

I looked at my list once more. "I think we pretty much got everything."

"That's good. Well . . . except for one more thing," he said, adding a wooden rocking horse to the cart. "All right, now we're done."

"Are you sure?" I asked, laughing.

He kissed me quickly and grinned. "I'm sure." We headed back toward the front of the store to pay. "Now, I think I should treat my wife and baby to lunch."

"Sounds good," I said, massaging my temples with my index finger and thumb. The headache that started earlier was now a little more painful.

"Are you all right, baby?" he asked, pressing a hand to my back.

"Just a little headache. I'll be fine."

"Are you sure? We can go on home if you need to."

I smiled slightly. "I'm sure it will go away in a little bit. Maybe after I eat something."

We continued to make our way up to the register when I heard a familiar voice say, "Hey, Hayden." We both turned as Debra moved toward us, pushing a half full cart.

I sighed. *Great. Another one of my favorite people. This day just keeps getting better.*

"Hey, Debra," Hayden said with a slight smile that I could tell was forced.

"How have you been, handsome?" she asked, grinning at him.

"I've been fine." He drew me closer and wrapped his arm around my waist. I couldn't help noticing the way Debra's expression quickly changed, as if she'd just noticed I was there.

Could she really be so clueless? I wondered. *Or does she just not care?*

"You remember my wife, Raine, don't ya?"

Debra's eyes narrowed slightly as she looked me up and down, her gaze stopping on Hayden's left hand pressing against my stomach, his gold wedding band glittering in the bright store lights. I smiled slightly and mentally shouted, *"Way to go with wedding band display, oh husband of mine!"* I casually rested my hand on his, the one carat diamond in my engagement ring sparkling like a beacon. It was a petty move, I knew, but I needed to make sure the signal came through loud and clear. Hayden was mine.

She quickly pasted on a smile. "Well, this is a surprise. I guess congratulations are in order."

"Thanks," Hayden said, smiling down at me, his loving gaze warming me through.

"So, Raine," she said, like my name left a bad taste in her mouth or something. "When is the baby due?"

"In April."

"Boy, haven't you two been as busy as bees." She grinned slyly. "You got pregnant pretty quick. But then again, you guys got married pretty quick too." She looked at Hayden and smiled, arching an eyebrow. "You sure it's yours?"

I softly gasped. Her words startled me so, I was speechless. In the past I would never have let something like that slide without a verbal comeback, but for the first time in my life, I was utterly and completely speechless.

Hayden's arm tightened around my waist. He was quiet for a moment. Then he took a deep breath and I knew he was tempering his anger. "Rather than subject my wife to your sour disposition any longer and risk saying something I shouldn't, I think we'd best leave."

Hayden's remark was so unexpected, I almost snorted. I was even more surprised when he smiled sweetly and tipped his hat.

"It was good seeing you again, Debra." There was no mistaking the sarcastic tone of dismissal in his voice. Without another word, he gently urged me forward.

Despite the pounding in my head, I smiled smugly at her open-mouthed expression and pushed the cart with one hand while I massaged my temples again with the other. The headache was getting worse by the minute.

Neither of us looked back at her but continued walking. By the time we reached the register, I was dizzy and spots were appearing before my eyes. I held on to the cart and leaned forward, squeezing my eyes shut against the excruciating pain.

"Hayden," I whispered, feeling my grip on the cart handle loosening.

"Raine," I heard his worried voice say, and in the next instant everything went black.

Trials are unwelcome but shouldn't be wished away. They produce a thicker skin and a stronger will.

Twenty-five

I slipped in and out of consciousness. When I finally awakened fully, I was lying in an emergency room bed at Roswell Regional Hospital with an IV in my arm. Hayden was sitting in a chair next to the bed holding my hand, his brow creased with worry. When his eyes met mine, he heaved a relieved sigh and smiled

"Welcome back, baby," he said, his voice cracking slightly. "You've been out for a little while."

"What happened?"

"I don't know, honey. You were holding on to the cart and the next thing I knew, you just passed out. I barely caught you before you hit the floor."

My free hand immediately went to my stomach. "The baby?" I questioned anxiously.

"The baby is fine, darlin'. Dr. Salem is having

some test run on you. They called him as soon as the paramedics brought you in."

"Are you sure the baby is okay?" I asked again, worried about anything happening to our child.

"I'm positive. The doctor listened to the baby's heartbeat and said it was strong."

I sighed, relieved. We both turned as Dr. Salem entered the room. The graying Indian man smiled as he approached the bed. "How is my favorite patient feeling?" he asked, placing a gentle hand on my arm.

"My head still hurts a little." I looked up at him. "What is it? Is there something wrong?"

"I'm afraid so," he said in a kindly voice. He rolled a small stool over and sat next to the bed, turning so he was facing both me and Hayden. "I got your test results back, and there is good news and bad news."

I squeezed Hayden's hand tightly as my stomach balled up in a tight knot. "What's the bad news?"

"Well, the bad news is you're suffering from preeclampsia, or toxemia as it's commonly called."

I didn't have to ask him what it was because a couple of my friends in Atlanta had had it with their pregnancies. "But until today, I have been feeling fine. How could it just suddenly happen like that?"

"Sometimes it just does. Every woman's body is different, and while some women gradually feel the effects of preeclampsia, it strikes others suddenly, sometimes in a matter of days, sometimes hours, which is what happened in your case." He flipped open the chart. "Now, we found a lot of protein in your urine and your blood pressure is pretty high. The heightened blood pressure is probably what caused the headache and the dizziness. Sometimes stress can trigger the symptoms and make them worse."

Feeling Hayden's grip tighten on my hand, I looked at him as he lowered his head and closed his eyes tightly. I heard him swear under his breath and I knew he was thinking about Jerome's visit upsetting me, not to mention the earlier words with Debra. I squeezed his hand back, urging him to look at me. When he opened his eyes, I gave him my 'everything will be okay look,' and he forced a smile.

The doctor looked up from his chart. "How is your vision?"

"It's fine now, but earlier it was a little blurry."

"Any pain anywhere?"

"My right shoulder hurts a little."

"Those are two more symptoms of preeclampsia." The doctor pressed his fingers against my ankles. "You've got a little swelling too."

Hayden, listening intently finally asked, "Well, what's the good news, Doctor?"

"The good news is since we've caught it this early, treatment will be a lot easier. Now, I'm going to prescribe a mild medication for the blood pressure that won't affect the baby. I'm also going to put you on strict bed rest. I don't want you to get up to do anything except to use the bathroom and take a shower in the mornings. That's it." He looked at Hayden. "Keep her down and don't let her do anything." He smiled and winked. "We both know how stubborn she can be."

Hayden grinned. "Don't I know it."

"Thanks a lot," I said sarcastically and he kissed my hand.

Doctor Salem scribbled a few more things down. "I'm going to schedule you to come in for a checkup every other week so we can keep tabs on your blood pressure. We're also going to do an ultrasound at each visit to make sure the baby stays okay, too. And the next time you come, we should be able to tell the baby's sex."

I finally smiled. "At least I'll have something to look forward to."

"Yes, you will, my dear," Dr. Salem said, closing the chart. He handed Hayden the prescription for the blood pressure medicine and gave me some final instructions. "In addition to your medicine, keep taking your prenatal vitamins. If you start to feel nauseated again, call me and I'll prescribe something for that as well." He stood and squeezed my arm. "You're all set. Now I want you to lie here for another hour and I'll send someone in a little bit to remove the IV. Then you can go home."

Hayden stood. "Thank you, Doctor," he sighed, shaking his hand.

"You're welcome. And don't you worry. We'll make sure this pretty little wife of yours and your baby stay well." He smiled at me once more and left.

When we finally arrived home, Hayden surprised me with his sudden protectiveness by carrying me into the house and placing me on the bed. "Now don't move," he said, taking off my shoes.

"Yes, sir!" I said with a grin and saluted.

He chuckled and kissed me. "You laugh all you want, Mrs. McKade, but you're gonna do exactly what Dr. Salem ordered." He opened one of the dresser drawers and pulled out a clean gown and handed it to me. Then he pulled back the covers. "You just slip that on and get into bed and I'll be right back."

"All right," I said, smiling up at him. I reached for his hand. "I love you, Hayden."

He knelt down on the bedside step in front of me and gently took my face in his large hands. "I love you too, baby. More than anything else in this world."

My vision of him blurred and I blinked the tears that filled my eyes onto my face. I was beginning to feel like I was going to be a burden to him because he had so many responsibilities all ready. "I'm sorry this won't be a normal pregnancy."

"Hey," he said, brushing my tears away. "Don't you be sorry. It ain't your fault. It's just something that happens sometimes." He wagged a finger at me, reading my thoughts. "And don't you be feeling like you're a burden. You're my wife, and it's not only my duty, but it's an honor for me to take care of you."

I smiled as more tears spilled down my cheeks. He again took my face in his hands and kissed the tears away. Then he finally kissed my lips. "I love you," he whispered again. "And everything is gonna be all right."

I nodded. "I know."

He quietly looked at me for another moment, his brow furrowing slightly.

"What is it?" I asked.

He shook his head. "Nothing."

"No, it's not nothing. Tell me."

He released a frustrated breath. "I just wish Jerome had never shown up."

"I know," I said, touching his face "Me, too. But this probably would've happened even if he hadn't come."

He raked a hand back through his hair and heaved another frustrated sigh. "Well, I meant what I said to him. I also meant what I didn't say. If he ever brings his tail back here, it will be a painful experience for him."

"I honestly don't think he will come back." I smiled, caressing his beard. "At least I hope he doesn't. The last thing I need is to have my husband locked up."

"I promise I won't break the law, darlin'." He smiled slyly. "Just bend it a little."

"You!" I growled

He chuckled and kissed me once more and stood. "Now you go on and change while I get you a pitcher of ice water and something to eat. I'm sure

Caroline will be here soon to see for herself that you're all right. I called her from the hospital and she wanted to know the minute you got home."

"Well, then I guess I had better change." I looked up at him again and smiled. "Thank you for taking such good care of me."

"No need to thank me, darlin'. I'll always take care of you."

As Hayden winked and left the room, I sent up a silent prayer of gratitude for the privilege of having him as my husband. I also prayed that everything would be all right with me and the baby.

Adversity likes to kick you when you're down. But love compels it to take a hike.

Twenty-six

If I was asked to describe the next day, I would have to say it was definitely the longest day of my life.

The morning was blissful because Hayden slept in a little later than normal. However, the blissfulness was ended abruptly by the ringing of the telephone. Hayden groggily answered it. It was David.

"Hey, David, what did you need?"

For the next moment there was silence. I didn't know what was being said, but Hayden frowned in response to David's answer.

"I really don't wanna do it," he said. There was a subtle tension in his voice.

I turned to my side to face him fully. It wasn't like him to say no to David, so I was very curious to know what he'd asked Hayden to do.

"Can't Tom or Lance do it?" he asked brusquely.

After hearing David's response, Hayden closed his eyes and sighed. "All right." He turned to see me staring at him and reached for my hand. "That's all right," he said to David before hanging up.

"What's wrong?"

He heaved a sigh and pushed a hand back through his tousled hair. "David needs me to make a hay delivery I don't wanna make."

"Well, where's the delivery?"

He looked at me, hesitating to answer. "It's Debra's place."

"Oh," I said softly, my heart dropping slightly.

He pulled me into his arms and buried his face in my hair. "I don't wanna go, baby, but David's back is bothering him this morning and Tom and Lance are taking over for him until this afternoon. If I could get out of it, you know I wouldn't go."

I pressed my face to his warm chest. "I do know." Taking a deep breath, I drew back a little. "You have to do your job."

As much as it bothered me to have him going to that woman's home, I wouldn't make it any worse for him by complaining. But oh, how I despised her at that moment! And I was sure this was just another excuse for her to see Hayden. True, she couldn't have known Hayden would be the one to make the delivery, but it still angered me that she was able to intrude on our lives this way. If I didn't know any better I would swear she and Jerome had met somewhere secretly and were conspiring against us, doing everything they possibly could to make us miserable. Leave it to my overactive imagination to conjure up such a dreary thought.

I burrowed myself deeper in Hayden's embrace, wishing with all my heart that I could go with him. It wasn't that I didn't trust him. It was *her* I wouldn't put anything past. I hated the thought of her being anywhere near him. If I had learned anything about Debra in the two times I'd met her, it was that she was a cunning and conniving little vixen who wouldn't give wrecking someone's marriage a second thought if it meant she could have what she wanted. And what she wanted was my husband.

Why am I suddenly letting the pains of the past come back to haunt me?

I had never had a jealous streak before, and at that moment I was completely surprised by my thoughts. I also knew I needed to stop them before they went any further. I sighed and murmured against his chest, "I'm okay with it, Hayden. Really."

"Well, I'm not okay with it," he growled. "But I guess I have no choice." He held me a little while longer and finally said, "I'd better get going so I can get back here and do some work. And I want to be close by just in case you need me." He lifted my chin and kissed me. "I promise I won't be there long."

I forced a smile. "All right."

Once Hayden was dressed, he made breakfast and brought it in to me. When I had finished, he cleared everything away and sat with me for a little while longer. I knew he hated having to do this. *I* hated that he had to do it.

"Are you gonna be all right?" he asked, squeezing my hand.

"I'll be fine," I answered with a cheerfulness I didn't truly feel.

"Well, Caroline should be here to check on you soon, but if you need anything before then, call her, all right?"

"I will."

He looked completely miserable as he stood to leave. Feeling the need to assure him that I was all right with everything, I grinned and said, "Tell Debra we can fix her up with Tom if she'd like. He's available. A tad more mature but available."

He grinned back. "True, but Tom is my friend. I wouldn't do that to him. Shoot, sugar, I wouldn't put that on my worst enemy, except . . . maybe Jerome."

I laughed and squeezed his hand. "You are so bad!"

"I know, darlin'. That's why you married me. Well, that and my great abs."

"This is true," I agreed with a chuckle.

He sobered. "I have to go."

"I know." I glanced down at my hand between his. "I love you," I said, looking up at him again.

He leaned down, pulled me into his arms, and kissed me warmly and slowly. "I love you too." He straightened. "I'll see you later."

"Okay."

Staring down at me for a moment longer, he leaned down again, kissing me once more before he left.

I quickly discovered that sometimes being left alone with your thoughts is not a good thing. Sometimes thoughts can be very dangerous to your peace of mind. They can lead you down a path you don't want to go, a path you don't even want to explore. Such was the case as I sat in bed through the morning. Hayden still hadn't come back and despite my best efforts, I was beginning to worry.

As I gazed out the bedroom window, my mind unconsciously drifted to Mama and her situation with Daddy. And subsequently from there my thoughts went to Jerome's infidelity. Just as Mama had trusted Daddy, I had trusted Jerome, but he had tossed that trust to the wind, leaving me wary of ever trusting again. And I hadn't, until Hayden.

Trying my hardest not to let these thoughts dwell, I closed my eyes and shook my head against the various mental images my mind began to conjure up. I refused to put Hayden in the same thought sphere as Jerome and my father. He was nothing like either of them, and they could only wish they could be the kind of man he was.

Keeping my mindset in that mode, I reached over and took a stack of magazines from the bedside table.

I flipped through a fashion magazine, and as usual I gasped at a few of the photos, thinking I wouldn't be caught dead wearing some of the stuff being modeled. I didn't think anyone could pay me enough to don some of those outfits. Some of them were clownish, and some bordered obscene. True, I had modeled some clothes that I would never choose to wear myself, but the outfits I modeled did provide ample coverage. If the outfit wasn't modest to some degree, I wouldn't model it. Thankfully, I did have a little say-so in that department.

Bored with the magazine, I was about to close it and reach for another one when a photo of a busty, blue-eyed blond jumped out at me from the page. Instantly, the woman made me think of Debra. I released a low growl and tossed the magazine on the floor. It was at that moment that Caroline came into the bedroom.

"Well, what's got your feathers all ruffled?" she asked, picking the magazine up from the floor.

I quickly smiled and swallowed my feelings. "Nothing. Just a little frustrated."

"Honey, if you're this frustrated about being in bed *now*, you're gonna explode before you have that baby." She smiled. "That's gonna be kind of messy, don't you think?"

I grinned and laughed, which is what I knew she had intended. I decided to let her go ahead and think my frustration was over being confined to bed rest. I wasn't about to tell her the real reason.

"Has Hayden been back yet?" Caroline asked, putting the magazine beneath the others on the bed.

"No," I answered in a monotone voice, trying not to give away my growing feelings of anxiety over that fact.

"I'm sure he'll be here soon. Are you ready for some lunch yet?"

"Sure," I answered, grateful for all her help.

"All right, I'll go and fix you something now." When Caroline reached the door, she turned back to me and said, "Hayden can handle her, Raine."

I looked up in surprise. I hadn't said anything, yet Caroline knew what was on my mind.

"You own that man's heart, girl. Completely."

I smiled and swallowed hard against the sudden emotion rising in my throat. "I know," I replied softly.

"Good." She smiled back and left the room.

It was almost dinner time when Hayden finally came through the front door. Hearing his footsteps coming down the hall, I felt butterflies inside. I had missed him terribly, even more so than normal. I looked up as he entered the bedroom. He smiled, but it didn't seem to reach his eyes.

"How are you doing, baby?" he asked, leaning down to kiss me.

"I'm okay." My voice belied what I felt inside. I

was happy he was home, but at the same time I wanted to ask him why he hadn't come to me before now. Instead I asked, "How did things go today?"

He slipped the dirty t-shirt over his head, sat on the edge of the bed, and pulled off his boots. "It went fine," he finally answered, not looking at me. He stood and headed to the bathroom.

My heartbeat sped up a little. It wasn't like him to be so quiet. Not around me, anyway.

"Hayden?" I said, just as he was entering the bathroom. "Is . . . is everything all right?"

He smiled and came over and kissed me again. "Everything is fine, darlin'." And without another word, he went to shower.

I squeezed my eyes shut, determined not to let my imagination run away with me. I trusted Hayden. If he said everything was all right, then I would believe him.

Hayden was unusually quiet that evening. He was loving and attentive as always, but something was wrong. I knew it deep in my soul. Something had happened.

It wasn't until he undressed and got in bed that I finally gathered the courage to bring the subject up. Inside I was still nervous. Actually, I was more than nervous. I was scared to death he would tell me something I didn't want to hear.

"Hayden?" I said as he reached over to turn off the lamp. He paused in his actions to look at me, and the wariness in his gray eyes increased my uneasiness.

"Yeah, darlin'," he answered. When I hesitated he said, "What is it?"

I looked at him for another moment without speaking. Suddenly everything I had planned to say completely left my mind. "Talk to me, Hayden." When the wary look in his eyes increased, I asked, "What happened this morning? And don't say nothing. You promised to be completely honest with me and I promised you the same." I lifted a hand to his face and he immediately squeezed his eyes shut. "Talk to me," I repeated.

He finally opened his eyes and I was startled as I witnessed a mixture of anger and sorrow sweep through them. Tears began to sting my own eyes. "Hayden, please. Don't leave this to my imagination. I have already done that enough today."

Tears filled his eyes. He gently caressed my face and it was another full moment before he spoke. "I'm so sorry, Raine," he finally said.

"About what?" I managed to get the words past the painful emotion in my throat.

His bottom lip began to tremble. "I just feel so ashamed." He paused and looked into my eyes. "That's why I didn't come back by today. I went straight to work because . . . I couldn't come home yet, Raine. I felt ashamed."

By now hot tears were streaking my face.

"Ashamed of what?"

He silently stared at me for a moment before he spoke again. There was so much pain in his eyes, I feared what he was about to tell me. I found myself bracing for his words as a familiar ache began to creep inside me.

"Never in my life have I ever hit a woman. I never let myself get that angry before. But today . . ."

My heart began to hammer in my chest, but for a different reason now. I pressed a hand to his face and caressed his beard. "Tell me what happened, Hayden. Nothing you tell me will change my feelings for you. I promise."

He took a deep breath, his eyes pleading for understanding, which I was determined to give to him.

"As soon as I got to her place and started unloading the hay, she came out." He grimaced, as if it pained him to even think about her. "Just like I expected, she started right in on me marrying you. She said a lot of things I don't care to repeat, and some things that aren't worth repeating. I got angry and told her to go back into the house and leave me alone. I said a few other things too that I probably shouldn't have." He stopped and looked away.

I sat up a little and took his face in my hands, urging him to look at me. "Tell me, Hayden. Tell me everything."

He gently pulled me back down and wrapped me tightly in his arms. "I'm so sorry, Raine. I didn't mean to do it, but I was so angry . . . and she wouldn't leave me alone."

"It's okay," I said softly. "Just tell me."

He took another deep breath, pulled back a little and again looked into my eyes. "When I opened the door to get back in the truck to leave, she grabbed the front of my shirt and tried to kiss me. She said . . . she said she could satisfy me in a way you couldn't. And I . . ."

I felt his muscles suddenly tense up. "You what?"

"I pulled her hands from my shirt, but she grabbed me again. I . . . I finally shoved her away from me and she fell. I flung her like a rag doll, Raine, and she fell hard. She hit her head." He paused and wiped his eyes. "I felt awful. I was about to tell her I was sorry and ask if she was all right, but she jumped up and started yelling, calling me every name in the book. Then she started in on you again. I finally got in the truck and left. If I had stayed there any longer . . . I would've really hit her, Raine. I know I would've." His eyes filled with sorrow again. "I've never completely lost my temper before. I can't believe I did it." He closed his eyes and turned away.

"Hayden," I said, pressing a hand to his face. "Look at me." When he finally did I said, "You didn't do anything wrong. It was just a reflexive action that made you shove her. I know the situation is different, but I had the same reaction with Chris when he kissed me." I caressed his face. "I know you well enough to know you would never purposely hurt anyone, especially not a woman. In fact, you champion women more than any man I've ever seen. She was trying to provoke you and you handled it the best you could. You didn't do anything wrong."

"Baby, please tell me you don't think any less of me for –"

I quickly took his mouth with mine, silencing his words, trying to take his pain into myself and his response was immediate. He pressed me close and hungrily accepted my comfort.

"I love you more than anything else in this world," I finally whispered against his lips "Don't ever doubt that."

He sighed. "I'm just sorry to bring this on you now when stress is the last thing you need. I'm supposed to be taking care of you, not making things worse."

"Shhh," I whispered. "You are taking care of me. No one has ever loved and cared for me the way you do. You're the best man I've ever known."

He held onto me tightly. "I love you."

"I love you too."

Hayden finally loosened his embrace enough to wipe his eyes and turn off the lamp. Then he wrapped me securely in his arms again.

I lay awake for a long while and mentally went over all he had shared with me. If surreal could be used to describe what had happened, that's the word I would pick. It was all unreal in a way, like it happened to two other people.

Once Hayden's breathing had become deep and I was sure he was asleep, I let the tears of gratitude come. And in that moment, I was truly able to let go of the painful memories of the past, because I knew without a doubt that Hayden would always be there for me. He would never let anything come between us. Not Debra. Not Jerome, nor anything the world threw at us. He was stronger than the world, and he would always guard my heart.

Anticipation makes one day seem like forever. But passing time always brings the unexpected.

Twenty-seven

For the remainder of my pregnancy, my days consisted of television, rented movies, crossword puzzles, books, magazines, and knitting baby booties and sweaters. Caroline taught me how to make them. I caught on easier than I thought I would and got pretty fast at it. Since we now knew we were having a boy, everything I knitted was blue. I never knew there were so many shades of blue. Caroline managed to find them all.

During the first few weeks, Caroline came to check on me twice a day, bringing me meals from her home. She always visited for a few minutes. While she was there, she checked the house and made sure things were done.

While Hayden appreciated his sister-in-law for helping, I knew he felt a little frustrated that he couldn't be home with me more. And after what happened with Debra, I think his need to be with me was even greater. He was still having a hard time with it all.

Hayden told David how he felt. After discussing the options, they decided to hire another worker to take a lot of the work Hayden normally did, including any hay deliveries that had to be made, and Hayden was able to be home with me for most of the day. I couldn't believe he did that for me. I was so tempted to feel like a burden again, but Hayden knew me, and he would have none of that. He assured me that his place was by my side. He wanted to be there for me. He was truly the most amazing man I had ever known.

By the time I finally hit the eight month mark, I felt as big as a house. I was completely miserable, and despite applying a little makeup in the mornings after I showered, I had never felt so unattractive in my life. I was sure that if I had been able to be up and active, it would have made a huge difference in how I felt.

I think one of the worst things for me for the past month was the restriction of physical intimacy. I missed that part of our marriage more than I could say. Hayden assured me he was fine and it didn't matter, but sometimes I couldn't help wondering if he just said that for me. Each time I started to feel that way, I immediately kicked myself for it. Hayden had never been anything but honest with me, and I knew deep down nothing would ever change his love for me.

All in all, it seemed that each new day was an emotional roller coaster ride. But I also kept reminding myself every day that it wouldn't be much longer, and I would soon have our precious little boy in my arms. I knew when that day finally came, all of the discomfort and emotional trials would be worth it.

Life is filled with both joy and sorrow, and we are meant to experience both. This is something I've always known. But Hayden would tell me sometime in the future that this particular day, and the week that followed, was the happiest and the most painful time he had ever experienced.

"Come on, baby," Hayden said, sauntering into the bedroom that evening. "I've got a surprise for you."

"Really?" I needed something to perk me up. I'd had a particularly down day. I had also been feeling slight contractions throughout the day, which Dr. Salem said was normal. He did tell Hayden to call or bring me in if they got any worse. Since I was only two weeks away from my due date, the doctor didn't see any complications with the baby if he came early. The prospect of going into labor was exciting, but I still had my moments.

Hayden lifted me effortlessly in his arms. "I'm taking my wife out for a romantic evening."

"Really?" I repeated again, excited about what he had planned. He nodded and smiled. I wrapped my arms around his neck and kissed his cheek.

He carried me down to the family room in the basement. I gasped in surprise as we entered the candle-lit room. My tear filled eyes were drawn to the floor where there was a large, thick feather bed in front of the sofa, facing the warm fireplace. It was covered with a white down comforter, and the two king-sized pillows were housed in white satin pillowcases.

To the left of the sofa sat a tray of Mexican takeout that he'd dished onto our good china. And there was a ballad playing softly on the CD player in the corner.

I finally looked into his eyes. "Boy, you sure have been busy," I said, my voice cracking with emotion.

"Yes, ma'am."

Mentally blaming it on hormones, I became so emotional, I couldn't speak. The little buggers were now working overtime. I closed my eyes and pressed my forehead to his as tears flowed down my face. He lovingly cradled me against his warm chest. I couldn't believe how wonderful he had been through my entire pregnancy. He had always made me feel so loved, and now this.

I buried my face against his neck. "I love you."

"I love you," he murmured into my hair. "I just wanted you to have a special night."

I drew back and caressed his beard. "Every night

I'm with you is special, Hayden. Every moment. But thank you for being so thoughtful."

"You're welcome, darlin'." He stared into my eyes a moment before kissing me warmly. He gently placed me on the feather bed and propped the pillows up against the sofa so I could lean back comfortably. He then grabbed the tray of food and placed it between us.

As we ate, we laughed and talked about what life would be like when our son was finally here. And by the time we'd almost finished eating, we had finally decided on a name for him. Dane Hayden McKade. Hayden chose Dane because it was his father's middle name, and of course, I chose Hayden because I wanted to name our son after his father.

"I can't eat another bite," I finally said, placing my plate on the tray. Hayden added his plate and moved the tray to the side of the feather bed. I scooted farther down, fluffed the pillow under my head, and turned on my side to face him. He lay down and pulled me into his arms.

"Thank you," I said, looking into his eyes and resting a hand against his warm chest. "That was wonderful."

"You're welcome." He pressed a gentle hand to my face and softly caressed my lips. "You know I would do anything for you."

I smiled, my lips trembling slightly from his touch. "I know."

We lay quietly gazing at one another and I literally felt his love radiating through my very soul. I was sure there wasn't a more blessed woman in the world. His thumb lingered on my lips a moment before he lowered his head and teased the corner of my mouth with his. I let out a breathy sigh just before his moist mouth completely descended on mine. I tangled my fingers in his hair and pressed him even tighter to me as his heated kisses melted through the very core of me. Each touch of his mouth on mine stoked the fires of longing inside me, igniting a roaring heat that seared me all over. His passionate affections went on and on. His breathing was heavy with desire.

After a while, my need for him was so great, I couldn't stop the painful whimper that escaped. When he pulled back slightly, I said, "I'm sorry, Hayden. It's just I . . ."

He put a finger to my lips. "It's all right, baby," he said as tears filled his eyes. "We'll have our day again. But for right now, I'll be content to just hold you and kiss you."

I sighed. "Me, too." I smiled and pulled his head down, and his kiss was mine again. I never tired of his kisses, and they never grew old, because each time he kissed me, the love and passion I felt for him was renewed. That fact always amazed me.

I was completely immersed in the fire between us when a sudden sharp pain caused me to pull back with a gasp. I closed my eyes and moaned.

"Raine? Raine, honey, what is it?" Hayden sat up slightly and leaned over me, pressing his hand to my face.

It took me a moment to answer, the pain was so intense. "They're getting worse," I finally said.

He completely sat up. "I'm gonna call the doctor." He started to stand but hesitated and squeezed my hand. "Just lie here and I'll be right back, all right?"

I nodded, not able to speak as another pain suddenly came right behind the other. I gripped his hand tightly and tried to breathe.

"Forget calling. I'm taking you to the hospital."

He quickly ran upstairs and got my slippers. He also grabbed a shirt and jacket for himself, and the *Escalade* keys. When he came back down, he took the quilt from the arm of the sofa and wrapped it snugly around me. "Everything is gonna be all right, baby," he said as he lifted me in his arms. I fisted his shirt in my hand and moaned as another pain came. He quickly took me out and put me in the SUV. After getting me settled, he ran back into the house and grabbed the small suitcase I had packed a couple of weeks before. By the time we were on our way, I was crying, the pain was so bad. I think Hayden must have exceeded the speed limit a couple of times over, because we arrived at the hospital a lot sooner than I expected.

Nothing in this life is sure,
except love.

Twenty-eight

The first half hour was a complete blur for me because the contractions were constant now. I was immediately checked by a nurse and an IV was inserted. When Dr. Salem arrived, he ordered an epidural for me. I squeezed Hayden's hand so tightly while it was being administered, I was sure I left bruises.

As soon as the pain eased and I began to relax and breathe easier, the baby started coming. This was the moment we had anxiously waited for. I felt scared, thrilled, and excited at the same time.

Hayden's voice was soothing against my ear as he echoed the doctor's commands telling me to push. Filled with a sudden burst of energy, I did push. It only took a few hard pushes to bring our son into the world. At that moment, I experienced a joy that could not be put into words. I was actually a mother. I had a son. A son by the man I loved more than life. We both laughed and cried. Hayden repeatedly kissed my brow and told me how proud he was of me.

Then he pressed his tear-streaked face against mine as we gazed at our son when the doctor placed him in my arms.

"He's so beautiful," I whispered.

"He is," Hayden said against my face. "And so are you," he added.

I turned and kissed him softly. "I love you."

"I love you too, baby."

I sighed, feeling that my life couldn't be any more perfect. I had everything I could ever want. My happiness was complete.

"Let's get this little guy weighed," Dr. Salem said. I handed our little Dane back to the nurse. The doctor came over and rested a hand on my shoulder. "You did great, Raine, really great. But I honestly haven't seen a first time birth happen that quickly in a long time. And believe me, that was quick."

Hayden grinned and squeezed my hand. "I guess he was anxious to get out here and see the world. He's just like his mama."

I smiled at him, or at least I tried to smile, and at that moment I realized something was wrong. I couldn't seem to get my face to cooperate. When the right side began to twitch suddenly, I looked at the doctor, then at Hayden.

The last thing I heard was the sound of Hayden's

frantic voice calling my name.

Just as you begin to feel all
is lost,
God in his heaven smiles.

Twenty-nine

Hayden

Hayden sat beside the bed holding his wife's hand and wiped repeatedly at the tears streaking his face.

Hours.

It had been hours since their son came into the world. Hours since the powerful seizure shook Raine's body, causing her to lose consciousness. Hours since he had been gifted with the teary gaze of her beautiful brown eyes.

He pressed his head against his free hand as the doctor's words again ran through in his mind. Returning his gaze to his wife's still form, his heart and soul were immediately hit with renewed agony.

Raine was in a coma.

When Doctor Salem had given Hayden the

news, Hayden had immediately fired a string of questions at the man. How could it have happened? Why had it happened? When would she wake up? *Would* she wake up? He had struggled with the doctor's straightforward answer.

"I don't know. All we can do is wait."

Wiping his face once more, Hayden moved closer to the bed and laid his head against his wife's shoulder, fingering a curl that lay against the side of her face. Then he softly spoke to her.

"I'm here, darlin'. I'm right here. And I ain't going nowhere." He sighed and fresh emotion filled his voice. "You gotta wake soon, baby. I need you. So does our little boy. We need you so much, Raine."

He raised his head slightly to look at her face. "Come back to me, baby," he pleaded. "Please come back to me." He pressed his face to her shoulder again and the tears began anew.

It was a nightmare, one he couldn't seem to wake up from. His beautiful, sweet wife might be taken from him. They hadn't even been married a year, and he could lose her. He couldn't bear the thought.

Surely God hasn't brought us this far to take it all away.

The pain was threatening to tear him apart. If he had been a drinking man, he would surely be sitting in the corner of a bar somewhere completely wasted, trying futilely to numb the pain. But if he did that, he wouldn't be where he should be, which was at his wife's side, being the kind of man, and husband she deserved. Not that he felt he really deserved her anyway. He'd tried to be worthy of her, though, and if she made it through this, *when* she made it through this, he would try even harder.

That afternoon, Caroline and David brought Hayden a couple of changes of clothing and his toiletry items because he refused to leave the hospital without Raine. He cried in their embrace and accepted the comfort they offered. He had asked them to call Raine's mother, which they did. They told him she would be flying in the next day.

A while later, the nurse brought little Dane in to Hayden and he held his son for a long while. He talked to Raine the entire time about their baby.

That evening the same nurse brought Hayden a pillow and blanket to use in the recliner when he was ready to sleep. He didn't think he would be able to, but once he slid the recliner as close to the bed as possible, he eventually gave into exhaustion and drifted to sleep with his wife's name on his lips and a prayer in his heart that he wouldn't lose her.

A new day is never promised,
but is welcomed beyond words.

Thirty

As I slowly began to awaken, I groaned from the pain of my sore muscles. Feeling something over my nose, I reached up and felt the oxygen mask. I pushed it away and slowly opened my eyes. Feeling a gentle pressure on my hand, I turned my head to the side, letting my eyes rest on Hayden's face.

"Welcome back, baby," he said for the second time, his voice cracking, and his red-rimmed eyes filling with tears. He pressed a hand to my face. "Baby . . . I was . . . I was so scared I was gonna lose you."

I looked at his face. His handsome features were haggard, and he looked as if he had aged several years. "Hayden," I whispered hoarsely, "what's wrong? Is the baby all right?"

He nodded and swallowed. He answer came out in a sob. "The baby is just fine, darlin'. He's eight pounds, and he's beautiful."

My eyes roamed over his face again and I squeezed his hand, startled by his emotion. "What's wrong?"

He again swallowed hard and continued to caress my face. "Raine, you have been in a coma for a week."

I was completely stunned. "What do you mean?"

He sniffed and wiped his eyes. "You had a seizure and you just went unconscious. The doctor said there was a chance you might not wake up. He said that it happens sometimes with preeclampsia patients." His eyes were full of pain.

I loosened my hand from his and pressed it to his face, suddenly understanding why he looked so worn. "I'm so sorry," I said.

He pressed a kiss to the palm of my hand. "I was so scared, Raine. I was so scared. Just when I had everything I could ever want, I thought you were gonna be taken from me."

I pulled him to me and held his face against mine, pressing my hand in his hair. "I'll never leave you, Hayden," I breathed against his ear. "I'll be with you forever. I'm pretty stubborn that way." I felt the sob that shuddered through him and choked back one of my own as tears stung my eyes. "I'm all right," I continued to whisper as I stroked his hair. "I'm all right."

Hayden finally raised up and looked at me. "I'm gonna be thanking God for that every day for the rest of my life."

"So will I." I sighed. "Hayden, I want to see our baby."

He smiled and pressed his hand to my cheek again. "I'll go and let the nurse know you're awake. Then I'll get him." He stood.

When he hesitated, I could tell just by looking into his eyes that he was afraid to leave. I squeezed his hand and again urged him closer. "I promise I'll be here when you get back."

A sheen of renewed tears appeared in his eyes. "I know." He smiled and a look of melancholy crossed his face. "We've beaten the odds so far, haven't we?"

"We have, and I have faith that we always will," I whispered just before he softly touched his mouth to mine.

As the warmth of his love washed over me, one solemn truth burned brightly in my mind and heart that would forever be a testament to me of the impact of the choices we make in life. At one time, all had looked bleak for Hayden and me, and I made the choice to take a chance on him and his love. I made the choice to stay. And because of that choice, I was blessed with the deepest love and the most wonderful life I could ever ask for. I had gone through some hard trials, but the end results were priceless. I had my husband and I had our baby.

Now I knew without a doubt that whatever trials life brought my way, God would help me see them through.

Family is the gift that is always beautifully wrapped, and you never want a refund or exchange.

Epilogue

I smiled contentedly and waved to Hayden as he walked beside the spotted pony with three year old Dane in the saddle. Our son's wavy, dark brown and auburn-highlighted hair shimmered in the sun. I could hear his giggles from the stable door where I stood holding our little Maggie, who had just turned a year old two weeks before. Her fluffy little curls billowed in the breeze and tickled my nose when I pressed a kiss to her forehead.

As Hayden slowly approached holding the reins, butterflies consumed my stomach. As usual when he was around the ranch, his shirt was hanging open, exposing his tanned muscular chest and stomach. I saw him either that way or shirtless almost every day, and it still never failed to make me feel warm all over.

"There are my two favorite girls," Hayden said, pulling me close and kissing us both.

"How was your ride?" I asked Dane as Hayden helped him down.

"It was fun, Mama," he said grinning just like his daddy.

"Well, your daddy is determined to turn you into a cowboy already."

"I gon' be cowboy like Daddy," Dane said, drawing a wide grin from Hayden and I laughed.

"Ain't nothing wrong with that, son."

"Well, I don't know," I said with a grin, looking up at Hayden. "Your daddy's a little rough around the edges." When he narrowed his eyes at me, I added, "but I guess that's all right sometimes."

Hayden shot an arm out around me. "Rough around the edges, you say? I'll show you rough around the edges."

"Hey, you two," Caroline called, walking out to us.

I heaved a relieved sigh and leaned back against Hayden's chest, cradling Maggie against me. "I'm saved. Thank you."

Caroline laughed. "Oh, I didn't come to save you. I just came to take my niece and nephew into the house for some cookies and milk. Would you two like that?"she asked, leaning down and tweaking Dane's nose.

"Yes, ma'am," he said quickly.

"Well, all right then. Come here, sweet pea," she said, taking Maggie from my arms. She took Dane's hand in hers and turned back toward the house.

"Ain't you an' Mama coming, Daddy?" Dane asked.

Hayden grinned widely at me before answering Dane. "We'll be there in a few minutes, son." He paused, taking off his shirt. "Right after I take your mama for a roll in the hay."

I started to run, but I didn't make it a few feet before he caught me. "Hayden McKade!" I yelled just as he picked me up and slung me over his shoulder. I could hear Caroline's loud laughter and Dane's giggles in the distance as Hayden carried me into the stable.

"Well, would you look at that. There's a fresh stall just waiting for us."

"Hayden, don't!" I cried, laughing.

"Too late," he said as he knelt and dropped me softly on the straw.

I couldn't help grinning as he looked down at me, a wide smile lighting his handsome face. "You planned this, didn't you?" I pressed my palms against his chest, instantly feeling warm all over.

"Now what ever gave you that idea?"

"Hmmm. I guess it would be the huge mound of fresh straw in this stall and the obvious absence of all the hands. But then again, I could be wrong."

"I would never do something so forward, darlin'."

"Never?" I said, arching an eyebrow.

His sensuous mouth curved up in a grin. "Well, maybe not never, but . . ."

I silenced his words as I locked my fingers

behind his neck and pulled his head down for a kiss. The heat between us was instant as his kiss deepened.

"You don't know how long I've wanted to get you back in here like this," he growled against my lips.

"How long?"

"Longer than I can say."

I smiled as my mind drifted back to the day he confessed his feelings for me in this very stall. I never dreamed that morning that my life would be changed so completely by the end of that day. I never dreamed I would ever feel so complete, so completely loved, and so blissfully happy.

I silently gazed into his eyes for a long moment. "Thank you for coming after me that day."

"I couldn't help it, baby. I was hopelessly in love with you."

I took his face in my hands and caressed it softly, tracing the outline of his mouth with my finger. "And I was hopelessly in love with you." I buried my fingers in his hair. "You were, and still are, the man of my dreams, Hayden McKade. And you will always be."

He said nothing else, but as he kissed me, I felt his emotions and knew he didn't need to say anything more. And the love that shone in his tear-filled eyes as he parted his lips from mine was proof that as long as he was by my side, the odds would always be in my favor.

About the Author

J. Adams has written books in different genres, but her main focus is inspirational interracial romance. She is a motivational speaker to both youth and adult audiences. In her spare time (when she has any) you can find her curled up with a good book and a healthy stash of orange Tic Tacs. She and her family reside in Utah.

Email: jewela40@gmail.com
Website: http://www.JewelAdams.com
Amazon Page: http://www.amazon.com/Jewel-Adams/e/B001TNK3GI/ref=ntt_dp_epwbk_0